BEYOND THE SUNRISE

DR. MARK JAY GANG

iUniverse®

BEYOND THE SUNRISE

iUniverse books may be ordered through booksellers or by contacting:

iUniverse
1663 Liberty Drive
Bloomington, IN 47403
www.iuniverse.com
1-800-Authors (1-800-288-4677)

ISBN: 978-1-5320-5878-3 (sc)
ISBN: 978-1-5320-5877-6 (e)

Library of Congress Control Number: 2018912254

Print information available on the last page.

iUniverse rev. date: 11/14/2018

To the victims of 9/11/2001

CONTENTS

PREFACE

It was a day in history that had a profound effect on the way Americans would think and behave in the future. Many still remember where they were at the time the jumbo jets crashed into the World Trade Center. Nothing in my training or experience had prepared me for the unexpected crisis of September 11, 2001. When I spoke to my father after 9/11, he shared with me that there had been three events in his lifetime that had a major impact on his life: the bombing of Pearl Harbor, the assassination of President Kennedy, and the attack on the World Trade Center.

As a licensed psychologist who was in clinical practice for more than thirty-five years, I worked as a therapist, consultant, educator, lecturer, television producer, and host. These positions brought me into contact with a variety of people from diverse backgrounds. It enriched my understanding of human behavior and provided me with the basis for the writing of this book.

The purpose of writing this novel was to familiarize the reader with post-traumatic stress disorder and its effect on an individual's total existence. The importance of effective treatment and its outcome on a person's emotional, social, and cognitive functioning are highlighted. My goal is that *Beyond the Sunrise* will help others understand how they can achieve a beacon of hope and comfort during a time of immense grief and sorrow.

I would like to thank my son, Scott Richard-Alan Gang, and my wife, Marilyn D. Gang, for their contributions with the preliminary editing of this book.

INTRODUCTION

When John left for work on the morning of 9/11, he did not expect to return home a changed man. This book is an account of how the events of 9/11 had a detrimental effect on the daily functioning of a fictional character named John.

A major focus of this romantic love story centering around 9/11 is John's struggles with post-traumatic stress and how it consumed his entire existence, including his relationships with his loving wife, therapist, friends, and employer. The reader will have a unique opportunity to go inside the counselor's office and directly observe John's therapeutic sessions.

One will become immersed in this story of 9/11 from John's perspective. John's attempts to overcome his inner demons will take the reader on an emotional roller coaster. Buckle your seat belt—it is going to be a rough ride!

CHAPTER ONE

ORANGE, CONNECTICUT

It was like any other suburban town in Connecticut within commuting distance of New York City. We were newlyweds, and it had been a blissful, fun year for us.

The night blackened the room with a veil of darkness.

I stretched, turned on the night-light, and reached over to kiss my wife on the cheek. Christina stirred for a moment, but she remained in a deep sleep. I sat up, uncovered myself, and stood beside the bed, admiring her. What a special woman. She was bright and beautiful, especially with her peach complexion, long blonde hair, and blue eyes that sparkled whenever she looked at me. She was everything I could ever want in a woman. She was bright, caring, and always sensitive to my needs. I did not want to awaken her, but I needed to be at the office early that morning. There was so much work to be done and so little time. When the stock markets opened in New York, I had to be ready.

I was looking forward to the evening. We would be celebrating our first wedding anniversary. I was leaving for work early because I wanted to arrive home at a reasonable hour. I had made reservations at our favorite restaurant, the Steak Loft, which was just outside of New Haven. I turned off the light on my night table, left the bedroom, and went to the sitting room. I felt a chill in the air, and my body shuddered. I reached for my robe and tied it around my waist.

I entered the bathroom, turned on the light, and closed the door. I approached the vanity and switched off the night-light. I turned on the shower, waited for the water to warm, and removed my terry cloth robe. For a moment, I gazed at myself in the mirror, which was beginning to be covered with steam. I hung my robe on the back of the door and walked into the shower.

The warm burst of water from the multiple jets was refreshing. I took a deep breath as the pulsating water traveled down my back to my buttocks and my legs. I lathered my body, closed my eyes, and thought of the previous night with Christina.

"John, you are home so late tonight," Christina said as she greeted me at the door.

I approached Christina, and kissed her. I put down my attaché case, placed my arms around her, and gave her a hug.

She said, "John, your big guy is awfully frisky tonight. I have been thinking about you all day."

I looked down. I was excited. "Can dinner wait?"

Christina looked at me and smiled. "I have been waiting for you for hours." She reached out to me.

I embraced her and began to passionately smother her with kisses. I eagerly removed my blue woolen suit jacket and loosened my tie. I tossed my tie, and it landed on the kitchen faucet.

She pushed me away from her and unbuttoned my white shirt.

I ran my fingers across her silk blouse, outlining her breasts, and removed her blouse.

She quivered for a moment.

My large hands initially fumbled, but then I successfully unfastened her bra.

Her nipples were firm, and her breasts were hard with excitement.

I caressed them with my moist tongue.

She sighed as she loosened my belt, and my trousers fell to the floor. She reached inside my boxers and grabbed my engorged penis.

I was extremely aroused. I lifted her, stepped out of my pants and shoes, and carried her, up the staircase, to the bedroom. I placed her on the bed and caressed her body with kisses. I told Christina that I loved her with all my heart and that I needed and wanted her.

Christina whispered, "You are my everything. I want you to come to me." She held out her hands.

I pushed her hands together and kissed them. I blanketed her with my body. I felt the warmth between her legs and slowly and gently reached inside of her.

She moaned with delight and directed me inside of her. She was hot, and her scent further excited me.

I was deep inside of her.

She yelled, "Yes, oh yes, more, more." I knew I had to delay, to keep her from reaching full satisfaction. I removed myself from her and moved my face down to her stomach. My tongue encircled her. Her clitoris was firm and moist, and I knew how to bring her to ecstasy. I felt the vibrations deep inside of her. There was not much time, and I mounted her. I placed my stiff shaft inside her and then moved my body up and down with precision.

"Now!" she yelled.

I felt her molten fluid, and I began to release myself, filling her with my bounty.

Our sweat-drenched bodies became one.

I kissed her, and we fell asleep.

I opened my eyes. The sensual contact with the shower water invigorated me. I reached for the shaving cream, stepped to the side of the showerhead, and spread an ample amount over my face. I dropped the razor on the shower floor and bent down to pick it up. I felt a sudden pain on my face and realized that I had cut myself.

When I stepped out of the shower, I felt something sharp under my foot. It was one of Christina's earrings, and I placed it on the shelf above the sink. I wiped off the mirror with my hand. Blood was dripping down my face. I placed a piece of toilet paper on the oozing cut and thought, *I better remember to remove it before I leave for the office.* At last week's staff meeting, my boss had commented on the toilet paper apparel I was wearing.

I had to hurry if I was going to catch the 5:55 to New York.

In the kitchen, I left a note for Christina.

> Christina,
>
> That was such an exceptional evening we spent together. You take my breath away. You are very special to me. I had to leave early, but I will call from the office. I am looking forward to tonight and will be thinking about you throughout the day. Happy anniversary. I love you. XOXO

I grabbed my gray suit jacket and walked out to the garage. I quietly closed the door and backed my blue BMW out of the garage.

The Milford train station was only five minutes away. It was early enough that I would not have any problem with parking, especially since the town had built the new station with plenty of parking spaces. I arrived with five minutes to spare and walked up the steep flight of steps to the platform.

A number of people were waiting for the train.

A friend called out to me.

I approached him, shook his hand, and asked what he was doing at the station so early in the morning.

Bill looked at me and said, "I have a meeting in New Jersey."

I knew Bill worked in New York. "What's happening?"

Bill became noticeably upset, and his eyes began to well up with tears. "Several months ago, I lost my job. My company was acquired, and my boss told me to pack up my belongings and leave the building. Those SOBs didn't care about my seniority or years of devotion to the company. It's been hard to find another job. I am either overqualified or too old. Who wants to hire someone who is forty anyway?" Bill looked down at the ground.

I was very concerned about my friend. I had not seen him for several months, and he appeared older. His hair had grayed, and he had gained a significant amount of weight. He was neatly dressed in a blue suit and white shirt, but he had a scowl on his face and dark rings under his eyes.

I asked Bill if he would like to sit together on the train to catch up.

Bill agreed, indicating that it would be nice to be able to speak to me.

The train approached the station and came to a screeching halt. The doors opened, and a burst of hot air hit our faces. *The engineers still have the damn heat blowing.* I spotted a pair of seats and motioned for Bill to follow me. It was sweltering and extremely uncomfortable. We removed our suit jackets and sat down.

We discussed Bill's situation at length, and I mentioned that he was too critical of himself. I told him that there were plenty of opportunities out there and he was bound to find something in the near future. I informed Bill that it was evident from the tone of his voice and general presentation that he was his own worst enemy. I emphasized that when he went on interviews his self-deprecating attitude was probably being conveyed.

Bill was very frustrated and conflicted. The weeks of unemployment and rejection had gotten to him. Bill was upset when he spoke, and his eyes filled with tears. He and his wife were worried that they were going to lose their house.

I asked Bill if the company had given him any severance, especially after all the years he had worked for them.

Bill anxiously replied that they had—but for only six months. He was overwhelmed by his circumstances. His eyes welled up with tears.

I thought it would be best to say something that might comfort him. I informed Bill that I would speak to the human resources department of the company I worked for to see if they had any positions that Bill might be qualified to fill. "Maybe they have contacts in other companies as well. Give me a copy of your résumé."

Bill was really appreciative of my offer. He placed his hand on my shoulder and smiled. He reached into his leather attaché case and handed me his résumé.

I reviewed it for a moment, nodded, and placed it in my pocket.

I was wondering how Bill's children were doing and asked him about them.

Bill noted that they seemed to be doing well. They were busy with school, friends, and homework. He and his wife were trying to shield them from what was happening.

I told him that he might have convinced himself about what the children had been experiencing, but he really had no way of knowing. He had assumed they were doing well, but my limited experience and knowledge in the area has indicated that children are extremely sensitive and very much in tune with their surroundings. They might know more than they were communicating with him or his wife. It was my feeling that Bill should have explained some of what was happening.

A tear rolled down Bill's cheek.

I told him I was aware how difficult things might be for him and the family but that I knew something good would come of it. I emphasized that he needed to think positively and success would follow. He had to believe in what I had said if he was going to move forward in life.

When the train pulled into Grand Central Station, I asked Bill if he would like to meet for a drink sometime soon.

Bill said, "Yes. I'm looking forward to speaking with you about your company's response to my résumé." He thanked me for my advice and appreciated my concern.

I told him that he did not have to thank me. As a friend, I was happy to help him out.

Bill looked me and smiled.

We put on our coats, nodded to each other, and walked onto the crowded platform.

CHAPTER TWO

NEW YORK CITY

I thought about Bill as I walked away from the Metro-North train. *How unfortunate for Bill to lose his job. The strain of losing his job has been very stressful for him. It would be great if my company had something to offer him.*

I walked shoulder to shoulder with the sea of people out of the crowded tunnel and into Grand Central Station. I looked up at the clock at the information booth and checked it against my watch. It was 7:35. I continued through the rotunda and marveled at the immense space filled with people traversing the area in all different directions. I was keeping up with everyone else and walking at a quick pace that would lead me to the subway.

I ran down the flight of stairs to the subway platform, reached inside my jacket, and felt for the résumé. I did not want to let my friend down.

I pushed my way through the crowd, stood several rows back, and waited for the downtown subway. The train was running late. It couldn't have been a worse day for it to be delayed. The platform was full of people, and they were backing up into the stairwell. I could see the lights of the train, and I wondered if I would have to wait for the next one. I was hopeful that the people in front of me would be aggressive while boarding the packed railroad car.

The train stopped, the doors opened, and the people rushed in like a herd of cattle. I pushed myself into the car and grabbed the nearest pole as the door closed. Someone hit me in the back with their attaché case. The train continued on its way to Wall Street. The lights flickered, and the sound of the wheels squeaking against the tracks as it came into a station pierced through my ears. The ringing in my ears abruptly ended as the train continued its journey. I hoped the train would not stall out. I really needed to be at the office. *Perhaps I should have taken a taxi.*

My worst fears were realized when the train came to a shrieking halt. The lights and the blowers shut off for a few moments, which felt like an eternity. The subway started to move and then stopped.

Everyone waited, but there was not even a hint of the train beginning to move to the next station.

I took a deep breath.

Finally, after a long interlude, the lights began to flicker. The train started to move through the dark tunnel, and in a few minutes, we reached the next station. The lights came into focus as we arrived. The next stop would be Wall Street.

People began to pour into the car, and I was sandwiched between several women. I felt a pocketbook in my ribs and tried to move, but my effort to reposition myself was futile.

The train finally began to move. It was speeding, and then it came to another abrupt stop. Once again, the subway cars went dark. There undoubtedly was going to be another delay, and people were complaining.

Why don't they fix these frigging trains so there are not so many delays?

The train began to move. I gazed down at my watch. It was a quarter to nine. I noticed the station lights in the distance, but the train stopped again. I heard a thundering sound, and the train car jerked. There was total darkness.

Something is not right. This is not just another train mishap.

Twenty minutes passed, and it was still total darkness. I began to smell smoke. I thought it was train fumes, but they were getting more intense. There was major concern among the people. The chatter was becoming louder. People were concerned and getting frightened.

Then there was a somewhat garbled announcement. "Ladies and gentlemen, there has been an incident on the tracks ahead that has affected our services. We are sorry for the inconvenience. Please walk carefully through the train toward the first car to exit."

The noisy disturbance fell to a veil of dead silence. I felt an undercurrent of tension among the people and was concerned that panic would break out. The auxiliary lights were flickering.

The passengers walked through the cars slowly and helped those who needed assistance. A general sense of fear and anticipation prevailed. I followed the others, and at the end of the car, the conductor helped people step down onto the tracks.

We continued on our way to the platform. The tracks were lined with policemen with flashlights. The police also assisted those who needed help and pointed us in the right direction. There was an older, gray-haired man with a cane in front of me. I supported him as he cautiously stepped down the metal stairs of the train car.

I followed the others along the tracks, but I quickened my pace once I arrived at the train platform. I did not want to be late for work. I was determined in spite of what was happening around me. The auxiliary lights were on at the station. The smell of something burning was becoming more intense.

I took out my cell phone, but there was no reception! I noticed policemen directing people to the street. I decided to take the north corridor, but it was blocked. I was forced to exit through the secondary exit to the street. I quickened my pace, but there was a massive crowd in front of me. When I arrived at the street level, there was utter chaos.

People were running in all different directions. Pieces of paper and ash were falling like torrents of rain from the sky. It was difficult to breathe. I made my way with difficulty through the wall of people and walked toward Tower One of the Wall Trade Center. Many people were running out of the building. They appeared frightened and terrified. Their clothes were disheveled and soiled. Their faces were covered with soot. They were shouting, "Help!"

I tried to enter the building, but when I was about one hundred feet away, several policemen directed me to move on. I could not get close enough to ask any questions. Firemen were hastily entering the building.

I attempted to access my cell phone, but there was still no service. Someone ran into me, and I realized that I should head toward the street. When I arrived there, I looked up. A ball of flames and smoke had engulfed the building. As I continued down the street, I turned back and looked up again. *Oh no! What the fuck?*

People were jumping out of the building. I heard screaming and thumping and splattering as they hit the ground. Sirens were blasting. A man ran into me, and I fell to the ground. Another man stepped on me before I managed to stand up.

The papers in my pocket fell to the ground. I reached for them just as someone stepped on them. A windblast encircled the soiled papers, and they went airborne. I ran after them and was thankful to be able to retrieve the papers. Then I heard a loud noise.

In the distance I saw a jumbo jet was heading toward Tower Two. *We must be under attack.*

There was a thunderous explosion as the plane collided with the building. Another fiery ball of flame encircled the building. I yelled, "What in the world is happening?"

I continued down the street, not really focusing on where I was going. The street was covered with ash, burnt papers, and other debris.

People appeared scared and terrorized. Several people were crying. Others appeared to be in shock. A woman stood by a building. Her stockings were ripped, and her blouse was soiled. Mascara ran down her face. Her hair was blowing in the wind. A man in a gray plaid suit was sitting on the pavement. His hands covered his face. Others were running down the street with horrid looks on their faces.

My body began to quiver. I was sweating profusely. I felt as though I was in a war-torn city. The streets were covered with the remains of what was falling from the towers. It was difficult to see several feet in front of me because of the ash and smoke.

I lost track of time. I wandered aimlessly down the street with the others. I quickened my pace. I started running. I was anxious and scared. The ground moved under me, and I turned around and viewed the unimaginable. Tower One began to move, and then it collapsed one floor at a time. With each ear-piercing crashing sound, it descended until it hit the ground. *Those poor people inside that structure,* I thought.

I ran for shelter and waited in a nearby building. Everyone who had congregated in the building wanted to know what was happening to their beloved city. A woman was sobbing, and another woman was comforting her. I have never felt so vulnerable. *How can this be happening? We must be under attack—but by whom?* People continued to pile into the building. There was another loud crash. The structure shook, and I heard a hallowing whirl of air out in the street.

I wanted to leave and make my way home. I was concerned about Christina and what might be happening in Connecticut. *How am I going to get there?* I could not anticipate what was going to happen next. It was an unsettling feeling. My whole life had always been in control. I was frightened and alarmed, but there was no time for that kind of thinking. I had to make a decision if I was going to see Christina again.

I pushed my way through the lobby of the building and out to the street. It was even more difficult to see and breathe. The debris from the falling building had taken its toll. There was a scent of burning flesh in the air. I gagged for a moment and covered my mouth and nose with a handkerchief. I continued down the street and away from the World Trade Center. I saw a man holding his bloody arm. A woman had her hand to her head and was sitting on the side of the road. Others were noticeably shaken.

If I can only get to Grand Central Station, perhaps I can catch a train back to Connecticut. It was a long, tedious journey. I walked through the streets quickly, not really noticing anything. I thought about my wife and wanting to be home. I looked at my cell phone, but there was still no service.

At Grand Central Station, I approached two policemen. "Could you please let me know what happened?"

The policemen looked up at me. One of them said, "The World Trade Center has been attacked. As a precaution, most of the trains have been canceled."

I asked about the trains leaving for Connecticut. I was becoming agitated, but I knew I had to control my emotions.

The policeman looked at me and suggested that I might want to check, but he was not too optimistic that my train would be running. He apologized for the inconvenience.

I gazed back at him and asked if there was any way out of the city.

The policeman replied that it was going to be difficult. It was his understanding that everything into and out of the city was not running.

I felt my stomach tighten. My throat was dry. I fumbled in my pocket for a stick of gum, unwrapped it, and placed it in my mouth. I moistened my lips with my tongue and asked if they knew anything about the cell service. I heard an ambulance in the distance.

The policeman informed me that cell service had stopped because the antennas had come down when the Twin Towers collapsed. He suggested trying a landline. The policemen excused themselves because they were being called to another location.

Without rail or cell service, what was I going to do? I wanted to be in contact with Christina. She was probably worrying about me. Several blocks away, I spotted a café. I was hoping that there would be a landline. *I could call Christina from there,* I thought. The café was dark and appeared closed, but I noticed a number of people inside. I opened the door and saw several people sitting at the counter. Others were at a few tables. An eerie silence filled the café. There was a dim light in the back of the room.

A woman slowly walked up to me and told me that she was sorry but that they had no electricity and were closed.

I asked if she had a telephone I could use.

She said, "Yes, but it lost service about an hour ago."

I asked about a restroom, and she pointed to the back of the room. There were several candles lit in the bathroom, and I soon emerged and walked by the counter.

I took a deep breath. I felt defeated and a great sense of loss. A general emptiness filled my body. I looked down at the floor and said, "The café lost service an hour ago." I took out my cell phone. There was still no service! As I passed the woman, I thanked her and left the café.

I did not know what I was going to do. Christina and I had no way of communicating. There was no way of returning home. I was among millions of people, but I felt very much alone.

I stood outside of the café for several minutes and tried desperately to compose myself and think about how I was going to resolve my dilemma. *I can't let my feelings consume me. I must overcome my fears and doubts and find a way home. Maybe I should have returned to the tower and tried to rescue some of the people in the building. When I attempted to gain access to the building, the police turned me away. Perhaps I could have assisted people in the street. Why did I just run? That was not the noble thing to do. It is too late now. I thought about all the people who perished.I will have to think about that later. I must find a way to get home to Christina.*

I started to walk toward the Henry Hudson Parkway Bridge, which would lead me out of Manhattan. If I could get off the island, I might be able to find a way home. It would be a long walk, but what else could I do? The people in the streets appeared dazed and mesmerized by the moment.

It was several hours before I reached my destination. A number of other people felt the same way, and the bridge was crowded. As I crossed, I breathed a sigh of relief. The sun was high in the sky, and there was a slight breeze. I was still miles away from Connecticut, but I knew I would manage to find a way home. I was determined, and I would persevere.

If the rails aren't running, I guess I can rent a car. I spotted a policeman and walk over to him. I asked him if could tell me where the nearest train station was.

The policeman believed there was one less than a mile away. He told me to walk in the direction of Ensall Avenue, which was off Johnson Avenue. There, I would find the Spuyten Duyvil Station. He pointed me in the direction of Johnson Avenue.

I asked, "Do you know if the rail service is operating?"

He thought so, but it was probably operating on an abbreviated schedule. "Only trains heading north are running. There is no service into the city."

I felt a sense of excitement and hope and thanked the policeman as he headed down the street. When I reached the station, hundreds of people were standing by the entrance. I asked a man if he had any idea how often the trains were coming into the station.

He did not know because he had arrived at the station a few minutes before me. The line was not moving, and it seemed like a train had not entered the station for some time. He was not very optimistic and said that it had been a rough day. "I should have stayed in bed. We're probably going to be waiting here together for a while. I'm Scott."

I reached for his hand, shook it, and introduced myself.

Scott appeared to be in his late twenties or early thirties. He was wearing a white shirt, gray trousers, and a blue sports jacket. He had a deep voice and was friendly. He appeared concerned and frustrated—but in control.

I said, "It could have been a lot worse, considering that the trains in the city are out of service."

Scott said, "You're probably right about the trains. Where are you going?"

"I'm hoping to find my way to New Haven. Where are you going?"

"New Rochelle."

That was a different rail line, and they would need to make a transfer once they boarded the train.

"Where do you work?"

I looked at Scott and said, "I was employed at the World Trade Center. It's been a dreadful morning, and I can't begin to tell you what I experienced."

Scott said, "I'm sorry. It must have been horrific." He had been in Midtown, near Forty-Second Street, when he heard that a plane had flown into the World Trade Center. He initially thought a small plane had flown off course, but the radio said there was a second plane. Both were jumbo jets that were hijacked by terrorists. From what he understood, other planes were involved as well. Before he left the office, he had seen dark smoke covering the sky.

The last report he had heard was that a jetliner had hit the Pentagon—and another had crashed outside of Pittsburgh. It was too early to tell if it was a terrorist plot.

The mood in the station was solemn.

For a moment, we both stood in silence. It was difficult to reconcile the series of events that had taken place. The line started to move.

That seemed to break the stillness. *We are finally moving. A train probably arrived.* I thought about what was happening. I wanted more information and wondered if Scott had more to share. I asked if he knew where President Bush was.

From what Scott had heard on the radio, the president was reading a book to elementary school students when he received word about the World Trade Center. He apparently continued what he was doing until he was whisked away by the Secret Service. He was presently airborne.

We continued to walk slowly toward the station and were several feet from the stairwell. We looked at each other and took a deep breath.

I felt a sense of relief. I said, "Perhaps we will make the next train."

Scott said, "Yeah, if another train is scheduled to arrive—unless that was the last train."

"You need to be a little more optimistic."

"That's kind of difficult on a day like today."

I said, "I know, but we need to have some positive energy."

Scott said, "I just want to see my wife and kids again. It has been a very long and frustrating morning."

I said, "Yes, it has been difficult, but we need to have hope."

CHAPTER THREE

ORANGE, CONNECTICUT

Christina turned over in bed just as her alarm sounded. It was eight o'clock. She took a deep and labored breath. She removed the handmade quilt and stood up. She felt dizzy and nauseous and sat back down. *Wow,* she thought. *What is going on with my body this morning?*

The sun was shining through the sheer curtains, and she greeted the day with a smile. Christina thought about her husband for a moment. It was getting late, and she needed to hurry to get ready for work.

She looked at herself in the bathroom mirror. She took out her hair clips, and her blonde hair fell gently onto her shoulders. Her turquoise eyes were bright and magnified by her blue nightgown. Christina approached the shower and turned it on. Several minutes later, the steam filled the room. She reached into the shower, felt the temperature, and adjusted the controls. She placed the showerhead on the pulsating dial. The warm bursts of water felt good against her body. Christina began to sing. She wished she had longer, but time was against her. Christina finished washing herself and her hair and stepped out of the shower. She grabbed a towel and wrapped it around her body. She took another towel and dried her hair. She finished the process with the hair dryer. She had twenty minutes to finish brushing her hair, get dressed, and grab a muffin in the kitchen.

In the kitchen, she noticed John's note on the table. A warm sensation filled her body. She would await his return home with excited anticipation. As Christina was about to leave, the telephone rang. *I don't have time for this, but I better answer it.* Christina quickly walked over to the telephone on the counter and picked it up.

"Hello? Yes, Mother, I am still at home, but I really need to go. I am going to be late for work. No, I haven't had time to listen to the television or radio. Please, Mom, I am running very late. I need to leave. What are you talking about? Yes, John left for work early this morning. I believe he had a meeting. No, I have not heard from him. Why do you ask?" Christina looked at the clock on the wall. "Yes, Mother. I am walking over to the television now."

Christina reluctantly picked up the remote control and pushed the power button. When she saw the news bulletin, it took her breath away. She sat down and began to cry. "I have not heard from John. Mother, I need to try to reach him. I hope he is all right." Christina stared at the television.

Intense smoke and flames were emerging from the World Trade Center.

She put the phone down on the kitchen table and covered her face with her hands. "People must be trapped in that building. I need to call John. Where can he be? Why hasn't he called me?" She heard a garbled voice coming from on the phone and picked it up. "Oh, Mother. I need to hang up. Goodbye. I love you."

Christina walked into the family room, turned on the television, and sat down on the couch. She tried to call John on his cell phone. There was no answer. *Maybe he is in a meeting and cannot answer.* She tried his office. There was no answer. *Where can he be?* Christina looked at the television, and she saw Tower One on fire. She walked over to the couch and sat down. Reality set in, and she yelled, "Oh no—he may be in there!" She began to cry uncontrollably. The telephone rang. *Maybe that is him? Oh, Lord, let that be him!* She ran into the kitchen.

"Oh, Mother, it's you," Christina said. "I thought you might have been John. I haven't been able to reach him, and he hasn't called. No, there is no answer at his office either. To tell you the truth, I do not know what I am going to do. Oh, that's right. Thanks. Yeah. I need to call work and tell them what is going on. Let me go. I will speak to you later. Love you. Goodbye."

Christina hung up and tried to compose herself, but she could not stop thinking about John. She felt an empty feeling in her heart and stomach. She was nauseous again and ran into the bathroom. She held her stomach and vomited. She washed her face, brushed her teeth, and walked slowly back into the kitchen to call her office. "Hello, this is Christina. Yes, I know, and that is why I am calling. My husband's office is in the World Trade Center. Wait a minute." Christina was mesmerized by the television on the kitchen counter. She saw a plane fly into Tower Two. At first, she thought it was a replay of the first tower. "I can't believe it. What is happening? I need to go. I will speak to you tomorrow. Goodbye."

Christina walked into the family room and sat down on the leather couch. She started to cry. *What am I going to do? What am I going to do? What happened to him? Was he in the building? Did he get out?* She gazed up at the television and screamed when she saw Tower One imploding. She closed her eyes.

Several minutes later, she opened her reddened, tear-filled eyes when the telephone rang. She felt dizzy and fell to the floor.

After several minutes, she regained consciousness.

She heard the telephone ringing and slowly walked to the kitchen. "No, Mother. I have not heard anything. What is happening is really disturbing. I think I passed out for several minutes. Oh, you have been calling for twenty minutes. No, no, there is no need for you to come over. I am fine. It was just the initial excitement. I will be all right. I just want to hear from him. I will feel better when I know he is safe and sound. I would prefer to be by myself. I will call you as soon as I hear something. Please let me handle this on my own. I know you are there for me, but I need to be alone right now. Maybe later. I will call you. Take care. I love you. Goodbye."

The doorbell rang, and it startled Christina. She looked through the curtains. Christina was surprised to see her neighbor. When she saw Carol standing on the other side of the screen, she opened it and began to cry.

Carol looked at Christina and asked, "Have you heard from John?"

Christina looked into Carol's eyes and shook her head.

She continued to cry as Carol approached her and gave her a hug. They embraced one another, and Christina felt comforted for a moment. She backed away and smiled, and they walked over to the couch. They watched what was unfolding on the television.

People were exiting Tower Two covered with soot and debris. The downtown area appeared as though it had been bombed. There was an army of police and fire personnel near the towers. Fire engines and ambulances surrounded the area. It was difficult for anyone to reconcile what was happening. The news reported about two other planes. One that had crashed into the Pentagon and another that went down near Pittsburgh. Each minute was like an eternity. They did not know what would happen next, and they braced themselves for the worst.

CHAPTER FOUR
THE TRAIN STATION

A cool breeze began to fill the air in the Bronx. The sun's warmth was beginning to dissipate as it began its descent.

Scott and I waited patiently on line for the next train. It had been several hours, and we were tired, hungry, and thirsty. We were wondering if the trains were still running and what was happening. We were determined not to let any doubt or fear that we were feeling control our thinking.

A period of time that had no parameters had passed. As I was gazing at a bird in a tree, the line began to move. Like a herd of anxious bison awaiting passage into the field, we followed one another to the front of the line. We did not know what our destiny might have in store for us. We entered the cramped stairwell and continued down a flight of stairs, hoping we would be able to board the train. A foul lingering smell that was overwhelming greeted us.

The approaching train appeared overcrowded. We were still at least thirty people away from the track. When the train pulled into the station, people pushed their way into the cars. The doors began to close. All hope vanished into a continuum that only had questions for us but no definitive answers. At least we would be partially shielded from the elements by the stairwell.

I felt a sudden sense of uneasiness and worried about my wife. I had not been able to contact her, and I was concerned and frustrated. I thought for a moment. *What will she think after she hears about the World Trade Center? There is no way she can know if I am alive or dead. She must be thinking the worst at this point. The news of the events must be plastered all over the television.* I took a deep breath. The stench of the station made me gasp.

I turned to Scott and asked, "Does your wife know that you are all right?"

Scott looked at me and replied, "Yes, I was able to contact her before I left the office. Our landlines were working at that time. It seems like it was days ago at this point. How about you?"

I answered him in a solemn voice, "No, I haven't been able to reach my wife. I am very concerned about her. I do not know what to do at this point. My cell phone has no reception. I tried a landline at a café, but it was not in service. You know how much we depend on these things."

Scott said, "What a fucking day this has been. I cannot wait until it is over—and I am at home with my wife and kids."

I looked at him with uncertainty in my voice and said, "Hopefully, you will be fortunate and have that luxury. There are so many who must have perished in that inferno. My heart goes out to them and their families. I can't fathom what my wife would have done if I was one of those individuals."

"John, the world today is a dangerous place. None of us can be certain about anything anymore. Who knew this morning when we left for work that we would be sharing this ghastly experience together? It is a major hardship for so many."

I turned to Scott and in a distressed voice replied, "Tonight, we were going to celebrate our first wedding anniversary. I was so looking forward to this evening, and now I do not even know if I will get home."

"John, who sounds like the pessimist now? If it gets too late or the trains stop running, you can stay with us. We have plenty of room. I am certain our landlines will be working—and you will be able to contact your wife."

"That is nice of you, but if there is any way I can get home, I would prefer that. If you wouldn't mind, I would appreciate it if you could give my wife a call." I reached into my pocket and searched for a pen and paper. "Let me give you our telephone number in case we get separated when the train arrives."

"No problem," Scott said. "I will call your wife. What is her name?"

"Her name is Christina, and I am certain she will be happy to hear from you."

"No problem."

"Thanks."

"John, where did you work?" Scott asked.

"I was at the World Trade Center, Tower One. I worked for Marsh and McLennan. What a spectacular view we had on the ninety-sixth floor."

"Oh," Scott replied.

"You seem very concerned. Is there something I should know?"

"You said you went to work this morning?" Scott asked.

"Yes, but I was late because the subway was delayed. Why do you ask?"

Scott hesitated.

What's wrong?" I asked.

Scott said, "I am sorry to be the one to tell you, but your floor was compromised by the plane crashing into the building. Being late for work saved your life."

I had not put the pieces of the puzzle together until that moment. I looked at Scott and my eyes began to tear. "That means that everyone who was at work this morning probably perished when the plane hit the building."

Scott looked down and did not respond.

My face was flushed, and I felt a sharp pain in my chest and a feeling of emptiness in my stomach. I sighed and said, "Why did this have to happen? Those poor people—and many of them were my friends. I wish I could have done something to save them, but I know any attempt would have been impossible."

Scott placed his hand on my shoulder. "I know this must be difficult for you. I feel a sense of responsibility in bringing this information to your attention. It must be very hard."

I stared into Scott's eyes and held my hand to my chest. "I just don't know what to do." I wiped my nose with my sleeve and looked away. Tears rolled down my cheek.

We stood in silence for a while, and then Scott said, "I wish the fucking train would get here. It is getting late."

I turned back and said, "Yes, it would be comforting to be home. Christina must be beside herself by now. There is no doubt in my mind that she must think I am dead."

Scott said, "It is too early to speculate about casualties. Most people have probably not given up hope. I am certain that Christina is awaiting your call."

I stared aimlessly into space.

Scott said, "Yes, you are probably right, my friend." He moved his hands toward me and appeared as though he wanted to shake me. I was becoming more withdrawn in relation to the heinous disaster.

He took a step closer. "John!"

My body shook, and I tried to focus. "I'm sorry. I just was thinking about my coworkers." I wiped my face. "I know I must look upset and somewhat despondent, but I have worked with these people for ten years. The thought of not seeing them again is mind-boggling. Some of us were like family."

He started to tear up.

"We used to stand by the copy machine and talk about our dreams and interests. What is going to happen now?" I looked at the people on the platform.

"John, no one knows what is going to happen tomorrow. We are thankful we have survived, and we have to make the most of it. This has been a horrendous situation and an episode in our lives that we did not plan for, but it is what it is. We cannot go back. We can only move forward. Those of us who survived must carry the torch into the future."

I stepped back and looked up at Scott. "You make a lot of sense, but I feel wounded. It is as though I was in a battle today. I was happy and content on my way to work. I was looking forward to our anniversary this evening. When I reached my destination, it was as though the world imploded. I felt powerless. I don't think I will ever be the same person again. I know I need to make every effort to pick myself up and carry on for those I love." I placed my hand on Scott's shoulder. "Thank you for being there for me."

I heard a screeching sound and saw the lights of a train approaching the station. I took a deep breath and prepared to charge forward.

Scott and I hurried down to the platform and pushed our way onto the train. I took another deep breath and squeezed into the car as the door closed behind me. I felt my leg rubbing against the person standing next to me. Scott was a couple of feet in front of me. Several people separated us. We nodded to one another as the train began to move.

People seemed excited that they had managed to get onto the train.

There was indistinct chatter. The pitch was escalating.

I tried to inch my way closer to Scott, but the train was too crowded.

On the side of me, a middle-aged woman was crying.

The conductor began to speak, but it was too loud.

A man shouted, "Quiet!"

There was no reaction from the people.

He yelled, "Shut the fuck up and listen to the conductor."

Dead silence filled the jam-packed car.

The conductor announced that he would be making unscheduled stops due to the cancellation of several lines. He would be announcing the stops along the way. There would be a stop at 125th Street for passengers who needed the Metro-North line. Further transfers could be secured at that stop to points east and north of the city.

I felt some peace and tranquility. I was heading home.

I looked at the woman next to me. She was still sobbing. "Can I help you?"

She shook her head.

I said, "It has been a difficult day for all of us."

She replied, "Yes, it has. I couldn't get to work today, and I did not receive my paycheck. My husband is going to be angry with me. I am afraid to return home without any money. We need to buy groceries. My children are not going to have food."

"Can't you pick up your paycheck tomorrow or the next day?" I asked.

"No," the woman said. "The building where I worked is not there anymore. It was destroyed when the World Trade Center collapsed."

I tried to reach into my pocket, but I made contact with the person standing next to me. I looked at the man and said, "Excuse me. I was reaching into my pocket for something."

The man shook his head and continued looking in the opposite direction.

I pulled out several bills and handed them to the woman. "This may help you a little, especially for food for the children."

The woman smiled and said, "Thank you. May the Lord protect you."

The constant bursts of warm air from the blowers on the train were unbearable. I was wearing my suit, and I began to sweat profusely. My shirt and underwear were clinging to my body, and I felt the sweat dripping down my face. I was so close to the person next to me that I could not even raise my hand to wipe my face. I thought about my wife and what she must be going through. She was alone at home and did not know my whereabouts after listening to the news of death, destruction, and despair.

CHAPTER FIVE

THE TELEVISION VIGIL

Christina and Carol were glued to the television. They did not speak to one another for long periods of time because they were consumed by the news. Christina had realized, on one level, that with the collapse of Tower One, the prospects for her husband's survival were dim. Christina was very conflicted. At times, she removed herself mentally and emotionally from the situation. Her detachment from reality afforded her a means to move forward. Sometimes, Christina sat on the couch in a state of disbelief. However, she would not let her emotions destroy her spirit. She began to dismiss any negative thoughts. She repeated to herself that she must forge ahead. There might be a chance that John was alive. *Maybe he ran an errand before work or stopped for coffee.*

Minutes turned into hours, and there was still no word from him. It was approaching three o'clock in the afternoon. There was a breakthrough of emotion that she was not able to harness.

Christina said, "What am I going to do? I cannot picture myself without him—and today of all days."

"What do you mean?" Carol asked.

"It is our first anniversary," she replied. Her eyes were swollen from crying.

"You have not heard anything. Perhaps that is a good sign. They said on the news that cell reception is out because the major antennas were lost when the towers fell." Carol reached out to Christina and gave her a hug.

Christina held her close. She felt so empty.

"Give it some time, Christina. Give it some time. He might walk through the door at any moment."

Christina moved her head back as she clutched her friend. She looked at Carol with astonishment and said, "That would certainly be a miracle."

The doorbell rang, and it echoed through the house. They both froze for a moment.

Christina rushed to the door with a sense of hope and opened it. "Oh, Mother, it's you." Christina felt markedly disappointed.

Gina was a gray-haired, short woman with blue eyes. She was wearing an olive-green dress and a dark brown raincoat. As she entered the house, she said, "I had not heard from you, and I was worried. I did not want to be home alone. I thought you could use the company. Hi, Carol. How are you doing?"

Christina was annoyed. She did not want to deal with Gina's emotional distress. She was having enough difficulty dealing with her own. Gina had a way of controlling the situation, and Christina did not have the patience or tolerance to react to her self-centered persona and the drama that might follow.

Christina was an only child. Gina had miscarried several times before Christina was born. Her younger brother died at an early age from pneumonia. Gina considered Christina a gift and cherished her. She was extremely protective, and in some ways, Christina resented it. However, their bond was strong—as was their love for one another.

"Mother, I wish you had called before you came here," Christina said as she sat down on the couch facing the television. "I really would just like to concentrate on the news."

"So, who is stopping you?" Her mother gazed at Carol and then looked back at Christina. She walked over to the chair. "You don't have to entertain me. I am not a guest. Did you eat today? Let me make you something to eat."

"No, Mother. I am just fine," Christina replied.

"You know you have to eat," Gina said.

"No, Mother. Enough with the food—I am not hungry." Christina knew she would have to take control or Gina would intensify an already emotionally charged situation.

"Either sit down and be quiet or you will need to leave. I want to hear the television," Christina said.

Realizing the mounting tension in the room, Gina decided not to say another word and slowly walked over to a chair, took off her coat, and sat down. She picked up a magazine, took her reading glasses out of her pocketbook, and began to thumb through the pages.

Carol looked at Christina and said, "I think I should go."

Christina quickly said, "No. That is not necessary. I really would like you to stay."

Gina looked up over her reading glasses, but she did not say a word.

Carol replied, "Well, perhaps a little while longer then."

The news was beginning to broadcast scenes that were quite graphic. Christina who was more interested in what was happening in the present rather than in the past. There were pictures of the plane crashing into the towers and videos of people exiting the building and firefighters and police rescuing badly injured individuals. Several individuals had been buried in the debris. Some of the victims were being interviewed.

A man was under a steel structure and could only see a small ray of light. He thought he had died and gone to heaven. He heard voices and called out. The rescue workers carefully removed the structure that encased him and set him free. He suffered a concussion and several broken bones and was carried to safety on a gurney.

Another man lost a shoe as he was pulled out of the burning building.

A distraught woman had been late to work. Her fellow employees were trapped in the firing inferno.

People were covering their faces with handkerchiefs to shield themselves from the falling ash and debris as they walked through the streets.

Christina and Carol looked on in awe and disbelief as they viewed the news. It was intensifying their feelings. Christina's anxiety was increasing with each passing minute. Her heart was racing, and she tried to call John. There was no answer. A tear rolled down her cheek.

Gina said, "Christina, we need to pray and let the Lord guide him home."

Christina said, "Mother, I am out of prayers. I just can't imagine what may have happened to him. The thought of John being trapped in his office and being burned alive is too much for me to bear." Christina began to cry uncontrollably.

Carol moved closer to her on the couch.

Christina held up her hand and motioned for her to stop.

They heard sirens on the television.

Hours passed, and it was getting dark. The sun had begun its descent, and the bright rays that once filled the room began to dissipate. Gina reached over and turned on the lamp.

CHAPTER SIX

THE SUBWAY

I was beginning to feel claustrophobic. I was wedged in like a sardine as I clutched the pole on the overcrowded train car. I was sweating profusely. Scott finally managed to move closer and face me. Scott was also overheated and wiped his face without making direct contact with the people around him.

The air was thick, and the stench was beginning to be intolerable.

"Scott, this is certainly a road trip that I would not have planned with someone," I said. "I am so tired and tense. I am so hot, and my clothes are fully drenched with sweat. You can wring them out."

"I know what you mean," Scott replied.

"Scott, how far are you going?"

"To New Rochelle."

"There is no telling how long that is going to be because this train is stopping at all the local stops to 125th Street. We will have to wait there for a Metro-North train."

"I can't wait to be out of here. I need some fresh air," Scott announced.

The train came to an abrupt stop.

"Oh no," I said. "Are we going to be stuck here for a while?"

The people on the train were becoming restless. There was no personal space, and it was too close for comfort. Several of the women looked uncomfortable. A thin blonde woman began to scream at the man next to her. He had reached for his briefcase and felt her upper torso on his way down. He attempted to apologize, but she continued to yell at him. He tried to move, but that was not going to happen. It was hard for John to see but he heard her relentless tirade.

Tension was beginning to reach a high point. Someone yelled, "Lady, shut your mouth already. I am sure he got the point. We have all been violated one way or another today. It was probably an accident. I have been pushed and jabbed ever since I got on this train. Calm yourself down or leave. I am certain there are plenty of us who could use more space."

The woman next to me was markedly upset, and her body was trembling.

"Are you all right?" I said in a soft consoling voice.

"Yes," she said in a troubling voice. The woman turned her head in my direction.

"I have no idea where my family is. All of us went to work this morning. They are employed in the Wall Street area. I have not heard from any of them. I am so worried."

I looked at her and said, "This has been a difficult day for all of us."

The train began to move.

I said, "Perhaps when you arrive home, you will receive some word about their whereabouts. Cell phone service has been out, and I have not been able to reach my wife. She is probably as worried as you are."

The woman looked up at me. Her bright green eyes were bloodshot, and her face was stricken with grief. "Thank you for speaking with me. I needed to hear some words of encouragement and hope."

The train made a rough stop, and some people fell into one another. Several people exited and walked onto the platform.

A voice said, "Thank heavens we have some room."

The cool air felt good.

Scott said, "John, we are almost there. I believe it is just a few stations away."

I must have fallen sleep for a few moments.

"John, it's the next stop."

I felt a great sense of relief as the train pulled into the station.

"Excuse me," I said as I walked off the train. "Thank heavens we are here."

"Not so fast, my friend," Scott said. "We do not know if the Metro-North line is running."

"How can we find out?" I asked.

"You are doing it. We just have to wait and see."

The cool breeze against our saturated bodies was not a good combination. We began to feel chilled, and there was nothing we could do. I began to shiver. Scott reached inside his attaché case and handed me a scarf.

I said, "No thank you."

"Don't you need it?" Scott asked.

"No, I will be all right. You look like you need it more than I do."

"But—"

"No, just use it. Really, it is fine."

"Thanks, Scott." I took the woolen scarf and wrapped it around my neck.

Half an hour passed, and several trains had come and gone, but no Metro-North. We were feeling discouraged until we saw a train in the distance. As it approached, we realized it was the Metro-North train.

CHAPTER SEVEN

TEA FOR TWO

It was getting late, and Gina said, "Excuse me. Would you ladies like some tea?"

"I think that would be nice," Carol said.

"Great." Gina walked into the kitchen.

Carol looked at Christina and smiled. "That is very nice of your mother. She is trying to comfort us."

Christina did not respond and continued to watch the news. Nightfall had come, and her efforts to think positive were diminishing. She thought about being a young widow, and the next knock at her door being the police informing her of her husband's fate. She turned to Carol and appeared hopeless and shook her head no.

Carol quickly responded and said, "You need to hang in there, Christina. Your mother and I are here for you. This is not the time to desert him. You need to be there for him—even if it is in your thoughts. Keep repeating to yourself, 'I am waiting here for you. Come home.'"

Christina looked at Carol and smiled. A tear rolled down her cheek. "Thank you, but it is so difficult for me. I am so exhausted and anxious. I don't know how much more I can take."

"You are expected to feel the way you do. If you didn't, you would not be human. Just take one minute at a time—and try to get some rest."

Gina brought in a silver tray with a pot of tea, two cups, and several cookies. She was worried and tried desperately to conceal her feelings.

Gina loved her son-in-law and knew that the chances of him surviving were not good. Christina had told her that John had left for work early that morning and probably was at work and died instantly when the jumbo jet collided with the tower.

Christina said, "Thank you, Mother. That was kind of you."

Gina smiled and picked up a magazine.

The telephone rang.

Christina took a deep breath and said, "I'll get it." She placed her teacup down on the table and ran over to the telephone. "Hello? Yes, this is Christina. Can I help you?"

The others looked on with guarded anticipation.

"You what! Are you crazy, calling me on a day like today. No, I am not interested in a free seven-day cruise for two to Bermuda. Good day!" She slammed the phone down and walked slowly back into the family room. "That man had some nerve calling me. I thought it was John. I am so disappointed."

Carol said, "Those damn telephone solicitors. They should be hung by their balls."

Christina stopped in her tracks, and Gina looked up from the magazine.

They all began to laugh.

"We needed that," Gina said.

"Yes, we did," Carol, confirmed.

"I am so disappointed," Christina said. "It is nightfall already, and I haven't heard a word." She sat down on the couch, picked up the cup of tea, and took a sip.

"I get calls like that all the time," Carol said. "I can't understand how someone would fall for that kind of sleazy marketing scheme."

Gina said, "He should have known better than to call you today."

Christina reached for a cookie and took a bite. "These are good, Mom. What kind are they?"

"Just some butter cookies I baked this morning while I was waiting around."

"Thank you for bringing them. It was not necessary, but I appreciate it." Christina finished the cookie, closed her eyes, and soon fell fast asleep.

Christina was living at home with Gina in Milford. She ran to the front door when the bell rang. John surprised her. She was not expecting him until the next day. Christina had a glimmer in her eyes.

Christina looked at him and said, "Our friends really knew what they were doing when they fixed us up. Last night was wonderful."

"They are better than the computer dating services," John said. "I was hoping we could go for a walk on this beautiful sunny day."

"That would be lovely," Christina said. "Let me run inside and tell my mom. I will be right back,"

John stood on the front porch of the older colonial home looking into the garden. It was the beginning of spring and the flowers had just bloomed. John stepped off the porch, walked over to the garden, and snapped off one of the daffodils.

Christina appeared at the screen door. She had changed into a yellow-and-white polka-dot dress and was carrying a white cardigan. She opened the door and felt tingling in her stomach. .

When John presented her with the flower, she smiled and said, "How beautiful."

John looked into her bright, blue eyes and said, "It is as beautiful as you are."

She grabbed his hand as they walked down the path to the sidewalk.

She asked, "Have you lived in Connecticut for a long time?"

"All my life. I was born in New Haven and raised in Trumbull. How about you?"

"Oh yes," she said. "I was born at Yale New Haven Hospital. This house in Milford has been in our family for generations. My great-grandparents lived here. It used to be a farm. See that school?" She pointed to the building down the street. "That was where I went to elementary school. In a few blocks, you will see my favorite place."

"What might that be?" John asked.

"You mean you do not already smell the aroma?" Christina pointed to the sea. "See over there, just past that white-and-green house."

"Oh, I see it."

The deep blue water of Long Island Sound, against the light blue sky, and the puffy clouds were picturesque. There were several sailboats and two barges in the water. A slight wind stirred, and there was a slight chill in the air.

Christina put on her sweater.

"Are you cold, Christina?"

"Just a little, but I should be fine with my sweater," she said.

John walked toward her and placed an arm around her.

Christina snuggled closer. "We should take off our shoes and run on the beach," she suggested.

They removed their shoes. Christina started to run along the beach, and John was in hot pursuit. A hundred feet down the beach, he caught up with her. He gave her a tight hug and lifted her off the sand.

They were both laughing. They looked into each other's eyes.

He moved in closer and kissed her.

She smiled.

He winked at her and placed her back down on the white sand.

They held hands and walked for close to an hour. "We better be heading home," she said. "I need to help my mom with dinner. We are expecting several family members. Would you like to join us?"

"I would love to, but my friends are expecting me." John looked down at his watch. "It is our card night. We usually grab sandwiches and beer and then go back to one of the guys' houses. Perhaps I could join you another time?"

"That would be nice," she said with a disappointed look on her face.

"No, really, I would love to have dinner with you and your family. It is just that I cannot disappoint my friends who are depending on me."

Christina smiled.

They walked over to the house and sat on the wicker rockers.

Christina said, "I had a wonderful afternoon. Thank you for the surprise. I am looking forward to seeing you tomorrow evening. Have you decided what movie you want to see?"

"No, not really. Did you have anything in mind?"

"We will talk later. I really need to go in and give my mom a hand." She stood up.

"Goodbye." John walked down the stairs to his car, waved, and drove away.

Christina opened her eyes. For a moment, she did not know where she was.

Gina said, "Christina, did you have a nice nap? You have been sleeping for several hours. Would you like something to eat? It is getting late. Carol left some time ago."

"Oh, I was wondering where she was. I guess I should eat something. I am not really hungry. I have only eaten a muffin and some cookies today."

"I will make you a sandwich."

"Thanks. In the meantime, I will catch up with the news."

CHAPTER EIGHT

METRO-NORTH

The train came to a sudden halt. I felt fortunate that Scott and I were standing in front of the train doors. They opened, and we pushed our way into the car. Others followed us, and we were sandwiched in again like sardines. For some unknown reason, the heat was on. Our coats were off, our shirts were unbuttoned, and our sleeves were rolled up. I had removed my scarf before entering the train.

"They can never regulate the ventilation system in these trains. It is like a sauna in here," I said.

"Yeah, and in the winter the air-conditioning is on," Scott replied.

I knew I would eventually arrive in Milford, but I needed to endure the long and laborious ride. There was a strange silence aboard the train. People were stunned by the day's events and were in a state of shock and reflection. Many were just staring into space.

I wanted to erase the day from my mind, but that was not going to happen. Over and over again, I pictured the scene at the World Trade Center. The sound of the people as they fell to the streets horrified me. *That could have been me. Perhaps a number of my coworkers chose that fate rather than burning alive. How am I going to move beyond the day's events? We are the fortunate ones. Why did we survive and not the others? I must try to go on. I have to for the sake of Christina. What will my destiny hold?* I shivered.

The train slowed down as it pulled into a station. I saw a crowd waiting to come aboard. A few passengers would be leaving. The doors opened, and the loud, chaotic rush of people replaced the silence. A difficult situation was becoming more unbearable.

One of the passengers yelled, "I can't move in any further. There is no place for me to go." The doors tried to close, but people were blocking it. An announcement was made, but it could hardly be heard above the confusion and loud voices. People were not moving out of the way of the doors. The train would be delayed until the doors were cleared.

A conductor walked the length of the train and supervised the doors closing. People had waited a long time and were frustrated and angry. The conductor kept repeating, "There will be another train. Please step back."

Scott looked at me and said, "I have several more stops before we reach New Rochelle."

"I wish I could say the same thing," I replied.

"We should be thankful that we were standing in the right place when we boarded," Scott said.

After fifteen minutes that seemed like an eternity, the train began traveling down the tracks. It was evening, and the lights in the car were flickering. Cooler air had filled the cars when the doors opened, but the oppressive heat was pouring in again.

I felt my clothes sticking to my tired body. I was hungry and wanted to be at home and in the arms of the woman I loved.

I wondered how Christina was doing. I knew she must be worrying about me. I missed her. I closed my eyes for a moment. The rocking train and the melodic clicking sounds of the wheels against the tracks mesmerized me. I fell into a deep sleep.

I was at home and had just picked up the telephone to call Christina. "Hello, is this Christina?"

"Who is calling?"

"This is John. I was given your telephone number from a mutual friend."

"Oh, I was expecting your call. I have heard a lot of good things about you," Christina replied.

"I was told very nice things about you," I said. "I am looking forward to meeting you. I must admit I was surprised about what I was told."

"What do you mean?" Christina asked.

"Now, don't get me wrong, our friend exaggerates sometimes."

"I can just imagine" Christina said.

"The only way we will know is if we meet one another," I said.

She replied, "I was looking forward to your call, but now I am not too sure."

There was silence over the line.

Christina spoke, "I am only kidding. I really would like to meet you and see for myself what is at the other end of the phone."

"I am glad you said that because I was feeling the same way. So, when can we get together," I asked.

"How is Wednesday?"

"Sounds great to me. How about I pick you up around two o'clock?"

"That is perfect," Christina said.

The train stopped short, and I opened my eyes for a moment. I closed them and once again began to dream. The train began to move.

I approached the house from the street. *That must be it.* I looked down at the address. *Yes, that is it. What a nice house.* I was somewhat anxious, but I was very interested in meeting Christina. I had never been on a blind date and wondered how it was going to work out.

I opened the car door and slowly approached the white picket fence. I reached inside the fence, unlocked it, and walked up to the front porch. I rang the doorbell and took a deep breath. My heart was beating. I wiped my sweaty hands on my trousers.

Several moments later, the door opened. A blonde-haired, blue-eyed young woman in a pink-and-white dress looked up and smiled. "You must be John. Just a minute while I will get Christina for you."

I felt a sense of disappointment.

She paused for a moment and then looked up at me. "Only kidding—I am Christina." She laughed.

"Christina, I owe you one," I said.

We both laughed.

She opened the screen door and reached out to greet me. I took her hand. It was so smooth, and her perfume was appealing. I smiled, and we walked down the stairs to the car. I opened the door for her.

She turned and said, "Gee, what a gentleman we have here."

"Where would you like to go?" I asked.

Christina thought for a moment. "That's right. You are probably not familiar with this area. There is a nice coffee shop about a mile from here. How does that sound?"

"It sounds great."

"Take a right turn at the corner and then your first left."

"This is a nice area, Christina."

"Yes, we love it here. The coffee shop is just down this street on the right side. There, just beyond that green sign." She pointed. "We are in luck. A parking space is waiting for you right in front of the shop."

"That is great," I said.

I backed into the space.

"You did that well. I am not as good as you are with that maneuver."

We walked into the coffee shop. It was a quaint place. There were several tables with white metal chairs around them. The tables were round with glass surfaces.

On the perimeter of the room were wooden booths, and there was a counter in the back of the shop.

A waitress greeted us and escorted us to one of the wooden booths. We sat across from one another.

"This is a nice place," I said.

"Yes, it has been here for years. Those pictures are from the early twenties when the shop first opened. What do you do when you are not sitting in a coffee shop?"

"I am finishing my last year at Yale. I am receiving my master's in business and marketing with a minor in psychology. A Wall Street firm has recruited me for September. How about yourself?"

"I am also studying business, at the University of Connecticut. I will be finishing this year, and then I plan on continuing my education for my master's degree in business administration."

The train stopped at the next station and jolted me awake. Scott was looking at me. "I guess I fell asleep," I said.

"I cannot sleep with all of these people around me," Scott said.

"We will be parting in two more stops," Scott said. "It would be nice if we could stay in touch."

I felt a sudden sense of loss. Scott and I had shared so much together—more than some people experience together in years. "That would be great," I said. "You have my number. I appreciate you calling Christina when you arrive home."

"No problem. It is the least I can do for you," Scott answered.

The second stop came quickly. Scott said, "It was nice meeting you. Too bad it wasn't under better circumstances. Let's be sure we get together again real soon with our wives."

"That would be great. I look forward to meeting her," I replied.

The door opened, and Scott hurried off the train.

When the doors closed, I had an empty feeling in the pit of my stomach. I knew I would miss Scott, and I wasn't sure if I would ever see him again. I was quite sad, and I did not know why I was reacting that way. He had been a perfect stranger several hours ago.

As the train began to move, Scott faded into the distance. I reached up and saw his scarf in the sleeve of my suit jacket. *I will need to give it back to him when we meet again.*

There was more room on the train. New Rochelle was a major stop. Many people had exited the train on its way to Connecticut. It was getting late, and I was thinking about Christina. I couldn't wait to see her. I finally spotted a seat and decided to sit down. As I made my way to the seat, I let out a sigh. I had been standing for a long time, and my legs and feet were tired. It felt good to sit after all those hours. *Now if there was only a bathroom,* I thought. *I guess I can wait until I arrive home. I hate using the restroom on the train. You have to be a contortionist to use one, and I am certain they are filthy by now.*

The telephone rang shortly after eight o'clock. Christina was listening so attentively to the television that she did not hear.

Gina yelled, "Do you want me to get the phone?"

Christina ran to the telephone, but by the time she picked up the receiver, the person had hung up. She was extremely disappointed and mad at herself for not hearing the ringing and began to cry. She walked slowly into the family room, and the telephone began to ring again. She ran into the kitchen almost tripping over her feet. "Yes, this is Christina. Your name is Scott. I don't know anyone by that name. You are not another telemarketer, are you? Yes, he is my husband. You met where?"

Gina anxiously ran into the room.

Christina had a surprised look of excitement on her face.

"On the train platform. Your name is Scott. He gave you our telephone number and asked you to call once you arrived home?" Christina's heart began to pound. "You mean he is alive and heading to Milford on the train? You just left him?" She began to cry. "I feel like I am dreaming."

Gina stood in silence with her hands clasped.

"I am so thankful you called. You have no idea what this means to me. Yes, I think it is a great idea. I would love to meet you and your wife. You will call next week? I will look forward to your call. Once again, thank you so much for contacting me. Have a peaceful night. Mom, did you hear that? John is alive. He should be here within an hour or two. I can't believe it. He survived the attack! It is a miracle!" Christina put her arms around Gina and gave her a hug and kiss. "I need to make him something to eat. He is going to be starving when he gets home. It was so nice of Scott to call. My dreams came true. I need to call Carol and tell her."

CHAPTER NINE

HOME AGAIN

At 10:06 p.m., the train pulled into the Milford station. I was standing eagerly at the door when it opened. The cool air hit me in the face as I walked onto the platform. It was invigorating. It was so good to be home.

I carried my attaché case to the car. There were several cars in the parking lot. I wondered how many people would not be coming home. I unlocked the car and sat down behind the wheel. I couldn't believe I was going to be driving home. This morning, I felt doomed and under attack—and now I was about to head home to be reunited with Christina. I reached over and placed the key in the ignition. When I turned it, the car did not start. I tried again, and it stalled. *What a time to have car trouble.* I turned the key again, and the car started. I took a deep breath of relief, exhaled, and smiled.

As I drove toward our house in Orange, I saw the town green and the stores and restaurants that lined the street. I spotted a few people at one of the cafés. A couple of policemen were eating doughnuts and drinking coffee in a car by one of the lights.

As I stopped at the red light, I nodded at the policemen.

When I turned onto my street, I sighed in relief. It would only be a few more moments. I felt a sense of excitement, but I was anxious and tense. I did not understand my feelings, but I attributed them to my long and dreadful day.

As I drove into the garage, I heard a loud voice calling to me.

Christina was standing by the door. She ran over to the car.

We embraced and smothered each other with kisses and hugs. I did not want to let go. It felt so good to have her in my arms. Our emotions were at a heightened pitch. I smelled the scent of her hair. Her body was so warm. I caressed her and wanted her.

Christina took one step back and looked up at me with tears rolling down her face. She said, "Thank heavens you are home. I cannot believe you are here. The news is so dismal." She grabbed me again and kissed me repeatedly. Tears continued to roll down her cheeks.

My first reaction was to retreat. I felt a sense of dread. I did not know why. I passionately kissed her and then pulled her back. "I really, really need to use the bathroom. It has been many hours." I ran into the house and headed for the bathroom passing my mother-in-law and acknowledging her along the way.

She winked and motioned with her hand for me to go.

I threw my suit jacket on the couch and headed for the bathroom. I looked into the mirror and saw my soot-covered face. I quickly turned away.

Christina was standing next to Gina when I walked into the family room. She smiled and said, "You look relieved."

"Yes, more than you can know," I replied. "It has been a long time." I walked over to my mother-in-law and embraced her.

She looked up at me and said, "It is so good to see you. Welcome home."

I smiled and gave her a kiss on her forehead. I looked at Christina and said, "I would like to shower and freshen up."

"I know what you mean." My shirt was also filthy and stained.

Gina said, "I know you two would like some time alone. I have things to do at home and will be leaving."

I looked at her and said, "Do you need a lift home?"

"No, dear. I have my car. I will call you tomorrow. Have a good night."

Christina said, "Have a good night—and thank you for comforting me today."

I turned to Christina and said, "She did not have to leave so abruptly. I did not even get a chance to speak to her."

"There is plenty of time for that," Christina said.

I walked over to Christina and said, "I love you and will be back after my shower. I feel so dirty."

Christina looked at me and said, "Take your time. While you shower, I will set the table. I have prepared something for you to eat. You must be starving."

I needed to be alone and replied, "Yes, I will just be a while. I really feel grubby."

"No problem—take your time." I felt different and distant. I did not even mention our anniversary.

I slowly entered the bedroom and undressed. I looked at my shirt. It was damp, and the collar was covered with black ash. I stared aimlessly into space. I thought of the men and women who were jumping from the windows and heard the sounds of their bodies as they hit the ground. I placed my hands over my ears and shook my head.

I left my clothes and shoes in a pile and turned on the shower. I felt so alone. I thought about Scott and knew that he must have called. *Christina never mentioned anything. Maybe she was caught up in the moment and forgot.*

A warm mist started to fill the bathroom. I felt the water with my hand and entered the shower. As the water covered my body, I felt a sense of relief. It was good, and I needed to try to relax. My thoughts went back to the city and the ash and debris. Could some of the black residue have been the incinerated bodies of my fellow employees? I began to cry. I could not help myself. The more I tried not to think of it, the more my emotions poured out of me.

What am I going to do? I am alone now. There is no one who can understand my anguish. I am exhausted from my grief. I am useless. I wish I could have done something.

I washed my body and hair. I rinsed off and turned off the shower. I grabbed my towel and dried myself. I stepped out of the shower and began to shave. When I was finished, I rinsed my face, looked into the mirror, and said, "That's better." I dressed quickly and went to the kitchen.

Christina was sitting at the table with a worried look on her face. "Are you all right?"

I looked at her and said, "Did you hear from Scott?"

"Yes. That is how I knew you were coming home. He is so pleasant."

"Did you happen to write down his telephone number?"

"No, but he mentioned something about us getting together—and he will call next week to set something up."

"That should be nice. He is a special guy. You will like him. I am actually looking forward to seeing him again. He was a great help to me today."

"It must have been rough for you," Christina replied.

"Yes—more than you will ever know," I said.

"Would you like to talk about it?"

"No, not really. How was your day? Was there any one here to comfort you?"

"Yes, Carol came over for a while, and of course, there was Mother."

"What do you mean? You sound sarcastic."

"She was not invited. She just popped in when she did not hear from me in a timely fashion. She wanted to be sure I was all right."

"That was considerate of her. It must have been difficult for her being in that big old house by herself."

"That is a good point. I never thought of that," Christina said. "I made you a sandwich."

"I am not very hungry," I replied.

"You really should eat something. It is getting late," Christina, said.

"I guess I should. I do not know what is going to happen."

"What do you mean?"

"My floor at work was wiped out. I don't know if I have a job anymore."

"You worked for a large firm. I am certain they have other offices. If not, you are good at what you do. You will find another job. Now is not the time to worry about it."

"I know they have other offices. There is one in Midtown." I looked down to the floor.

"You ought to call them in the morning and let them know you survived the heinous attack."

"That is probably a good idea," I said.

I was depressed, and it was more than just being tired and worn out by the long day. I was just staring at the wall, and I rarely made eye contact with her.

Christina said, "I heard on television this evening that some of the companies are offering counseling."

I looked at her with a disgusted look. I angrily said, "Are you saying you think I need counseling?"

She looked at me with tears in her eyes. "John, you evidently went through pure hell today. I am not certain of the extent of what happened to you. Sometimes it is helpful to speak to someone who is familiar with that type of trauma."

I looked at Christina and said, "How about you? You have gone through a hard day not knowing if I was living or dead. I could have easily been at the office if it wasn't for the fucking train being late."

"Perhaps they have treatment for spouses as well," Christina suggested.

I was enraged. "I am not crazy, and I don't need to speak to some stranger about my feelings." I stood up. "Enough with this bullshit. I am tired and going to bed. If you want to talk to someone, go right ahead. Just leave me out of it. I don't need that kind of help. I am fine the way I am." I left the kitchen, leaving Christina at the table.

She sat at the table for several hours, crying and thinking.

Christina walked into the bedroom at one o'clock. The light was off, and I was snoring. She changed into her nightgown, quietly pulled back the covers, and climbed into bed.

CHAPTER TEN

THE NIGHTMARE

I had difficulty sleeping, and I was extremely restless. I kept on tossing and turning. At times, I would call out—but then I was silent. I was dreaming.

I was at my office at the World Trade Center. "Excuse me, everyone. I am sorry I am late for the meeting. The subway stalled out again this morning. I wish they would hire someone competent to repair the trains. They certainly charge enough."

Jayne said, "John, it has been that way for years—and I am certain it will be that way for years to come. We just have to work around it. Anyway, look at the bright side. It is a gorgeous day, and you have a great earnings report to share with your colleagues. Right?"

"Good morning—and a beautiful one it is," I said. "I am happy to report that our earnings continue to grow. The new accounts brought in by Bill and Chris have significantly added to our bottom line. Congratulations, guys!"

I took a sip of the freshly brewed coffee and reached for a doughnut. "Thanks, Mary, for stopping at the bakery before the meeting." I looked out of the window. "What is that?"

Everyone around the conference table turned to see what was happening. A jumbo jet was heading right toward the building. As it approached, we ducked beneath the conference table. There was a loud explosion and then flames. I could feel the heat encompassing my body. It was getting hotter, and I could smell burning flesh. The temperature was rising. I looked out beyond the enclosed conference room, which was now a frame of broken glass. People were bleeding and their bodies were engulfed with flames. There were body parts scattered around the room. I tried to free myself from the confines of the table, but the flames trapped me. If I moved, I would be burned alive. The flames were approaching. The heat was insurmountable. I could not move. I began to yell for help, but there was no one there to rescue me. I yelled and yelled. I could not breathe. My lungs were being filled with smoke and ash.

"John, wake up."

I stirred for a moment and yelled, "Help me! I am dying!"

"Wake up. You are having a nightmare," Christina said.

I opened my eyes. I was sweating profusely, and I did not know where I was.

"It is okay. You are home." Christina reached over and turned on the lamp on the night table.

"I am home?" I stared at Christina, but I did not make eye contact.

"Yes, you are with me—and you are safe."

I gazed into her eyes and said in rapid succession, "I was there, and the office was burning. I could not do anything. I was trapped. I was helpless. I was going to die with everyone else."

She gave me a hug. "You are with me, and you are the safe. You were having a bad dream."

"But it was so real. I could smell the burning flesh."

"I know, but it was only a dream. You are safe now."

"I did want to help. I really did, but I couldn't."

"I know, sweetheart. I know you wanted to be there for your fellow workers."

I began to cry. "I did—I really did."

"It was just something beyond your control. You are here now. Why don't you change your pajamas? I will make you some tea."

"That would be nice." I looked around the room in disbelief.

I walked over to my dresser and took out a clean set of pajamas. I looked at the floor and saw my soiled clothes from the previous night.

I looked away and walked into the bathroom. I decided to rinse off in the shower. I felt dirty and wanted to clean the perspiration from my body. The warm water always made me feel better.

I put on my pajamas and my terry cloth robe and went to the kitchen.

Christina was clearing my uneaten sandwich from the table as the teakettle began to whistle. She lifted it from the stove and poured two cups of tea. She put several butter cookies on a plate and carried them to the table.

I said, "Thank you, Christina, for being here for me. I missed you today. I thought about you often, and I was looking forward to celebrating our anniversary before I left for work this morning."

"Perhaps we will be celebrating something else."

"What do you mean?"

"I will know more in the morning."

"Is it something you wish to share with me?"

"I was going to wait, but I guess this is as good a time as any. I have not been feeling well in the morning. I have been dizzy and nauseous."

"Oh!"

"Yes, so I have decided to take a pregnancy test."

"What?" I replied.

"Yes, a pregnancy test. I think I may be pregnant."

I was removed from my thoughts for a moment. "What are you waiting for? Why not do it now?"

"Now? Really?"

"Yes, why not?" I looked into her face and smiled.

"Let's go into the bathroom," Christina said.

In the bathroom, Christina opened the vanity, took out the pregnancy kit, and placed a urine sample on the indicator.

I joined her in the bathroom, and we waited for several moments. We looked at each other and then at the testing stick. It was positive.

"I guess we are pregnant," Christina said with a grin.

"I guess we are," I said.

We walked into the kitchen and sat down at the table. I reached for a cookie and lifted my teacup. "Here's to us and junior," I said.

CHAPTER ELEVEN
THE MORNING AFTER

Christina awakened shortly after dawn. She was excited about her news, as well as concerned about John, and had difficulty sleeping. During the night, she awoke several times to keep a watchful eye on him. He was in a deep sleep and appeared to have had a restful night.

Christina put on her robe on and entered the bathroom. It was a good morning. She wasn't nauseous, and she was famished. She had not eaten much the previous day and was looking forward to a muffin and tea.

Christina washed her face and brushed her hair. She walked to the kitchen, took out a blueberry muffin, and placed the teakettle on the stove. She opened the wooden cabinet and reached for a plate. Christina tightened her robe as she sat down at the kitchen table, placing the plate in front of her.

She looked out of the window and thought about her husband. Christina was hoping he would be all right, but she had some strong doubts. She had watched the horrible events on television and realized that John had actually experienced them. How terrible and traumatic it must have been for him. He was fortunate to have met Scott and shared some of his feelings, but she was certain that he had buried many more of them deep in his mind.

John just wasn't the same until she told him about the pregnancy test. He was typically an outgoing and friendly person, with an even mood. He rarely got upset. The yelling and anger last night was not typical of his behavior. Christina didn't know how to handle the situation. Her attempt to speak to him had failed.

She placed her hand on her stomach and smiled. She gazed at a robin on a tree branch and thought, *I am carrying my husband's baby—maybe this will make things better.* Christina walked over to the stove and lifted the teakettle before the boiling water had a chance to generate the whistle and disturb John. She poured the tea into a brown mug, reached for a magazine on the counter, and sat down at the table.

At nine o'clock, Christina heard some stirring in the bedroom. It sounded like the shower. She walked into the bedroom, and the bathroom door was shut. She knocked on the door and walked into the steam-filled room. "Good morning, John."

He peeked out of the shower and smiled.

She was enamored by his appearance. He was a handsome, well-built man with blue eyes and light brown curly hair. Christina took off her nightgown and let it drop to the ground. Her beautiful breasts were firm. She walked over to the shower, opened the door, and stepped in. "I thought you would like a back wash."

"That would be nice."

Christina reached for the soap and began to lather his back.

He felt her hands slowly moving down his back to his waist and was becoming excited and aroused. She turned his body around and went down on him.

"That feels good," John said.

She looked up at him and smiled.

He began to rub her back, and then she faced him. He lifted her up. She wrapped her legs around his waist, and he entered her. "Are you all right?"

"Yes, silly. I am fine."

They continued passionately together.

He was very excited, and his movements increased in intensity.

Christina was breathing heavily.

John let himself go and with each pulsating movement he felt Christina's contractions. He held her close to him for several minutes. He kissed her neck.

She caressed him with her warm, moist lips several times. She said, "I love you and am so thankful that we are together."

John left the shower, and Christina finished washing. When she emerged, he was drying his hair. He handed her a towel and gave her a kiss on the cheek.

John headed for the kitchen.

I walked into the kitchen, turned on the television, and sat down at the table. My bathrobe was wrapped loosely around me.

The news was replaying the crashing of the jumbo jet planes into the World Trade Center. My body stiffened. I felt tightness in my stomach and emptiness in my heart. I stared aimlessly into space.

Christina walked into the kitchen and turned off the television.

I had tears in my eyes.

Christina stood in front of me and tried to make eye contact with me. "What would you like for breakfast, John?"

I did not respond.

"John, are you hungry?"

I slowly moved my head in a robotic manner. "I was just looking at the television. All those people in those buildings," I said in a soft voice.

The telephone rang.

"John, can you get that? My hands are wet."

I paused for a moment and then answered the telephone.

"Good morning, Mom. I am doing well, I guess. I was just watching television, but we decided to have some breakfast. Christina is at the sink. Oh, okay. You can speak to her later. Thanks for calling."

I was feeling all alone in the world. My parents had died several years ago before Christina came into my life. So when I met Gina, I developed a close and endearing relationship with her. My parents had been involved in a fatal automobile accident and died instantly. The event was very difficult for me. I had grown up as an only child. It had taken me quite a while to work through the trauma and my feelings of loss, but I managed to it.

My education and work were my salvation. I loved my job and the people who worked with me. I was respected and excelled at what I did. I was promoted several times and took my work seriously. I often left for work early in the morning. It was this side of a miracle that I wasn't in the World Trade Center when the plane crashed into the building. *The loss of my job and the people I worked with will leave a major void in my life. The bereavement will be difficult. It will take me a long time to work through the major issues that are confronting me.*

Christina seemed confused and concerned about me. Without counseling of some kind, my recovery would be slow and difficult. I could be stubborn and difficult. When I lost my parents, I withdrew for months. It took a lot of effort and support from others to get through the grieving process. People were very patient and understanding, but I was much younger then.

Christina left me alone for hours to deal with what she called my "demons." I managed to go to work, and that major distraction helped me move on with my life. I felt like I was moving on with my life.

I had accomplished a great deal at work in a relatively short period of time, but whatever strength I had managed to amass was crushed. I was burdened by something heavy.

I sat down at the table. "Eggs? Yes, eggs would be nice, Christina. Thank you for asking."

"No problem, John. How would you like them fixed?

"Over easy would be great."

Christina took the eggs out of the refrigerator and placed them on the counter. One rolled onto the floor. "Oh shoot!"

I sat motionless.

"John, can you please give me a hand?"

"Certainly," I walked over to the stove, barely missing the splattered egg.

"No, silly. I dropped an egg on the floor."

"Oh, I must have missed that. I was thinking about Scott." I grabbed a paper towel and wiped up the egg. "I wonder what he is doing today. I am not certain if his place of employment is open."

Christina stood in silence and began to fry the eggs.

"Scott worked near the World Trade Center, but I am not sure how close he was to the building. Do you know several buildings were severely damaged and will probably need to be demolished?"

"Is that so?"

"Too bad I don't have his telephone number. I would like to give him a call."

Christina finished cooking the eggs, grabbed two pieces of toast, and walked over to the table.

"You know, it was just by chance that we met. At first, I did not care for some of his remarks. However, I grew to like him. There was just something about him that was appealing. I can't place my finger on it, but he seemed to understand me."

I dipped my toast in the yolk and began to eat. "Thank you again, Christina. This is good."

"No problem, John. I am glad you are enjoying what I prepared for you."

"Christina, do you think you should call your mother and share our news with her?"

The telephone began to ring. Christina walked over to the phone and picked it up. "Hello? Yes, this is his residence. May I ask who is calling? Yes, he is at home. I will get him for you."

Christina walked over to me and handed me the telephone. "It is Mr. Lawson from Marsh and McLennan."

I took a deep breath and thought for a moment. *Maybe there was an error and the plane hit another floor and my fellow employees managed to escape.*

"Yes, this is John. I did go to work yesterday, but I was late because of the subway. You know how that is. I wanted to get there early to prepare for the meeting. Oh, I see."

Christina sat in silence for a while.

A tear rolled down my cheek and onto my robe. "Yes, it has been very difficult for me. I have thought about them often. My heart goes out to their families. I wish I could have done something, but when

I arrived at the tower, the police were blocking people from entering the building. Yes, I fully understand your predicament. I can make myself available. Tomorrow will be fine. About ten thirty. Yes, I will be there. Goodbye then. You take care."

I hung up the telephone and continued to eat. I looked up at Christina and said, "That was my boss. He had a meeting yesterday out of the office and was calling everyone to determine the casualties. It appears that most of the employees were present. Only a handful of us were out on assignment or late for work. The rest have perished." I stopped for a moment, looked away, and began to cry.

Christina walked over to me and gave me a hug.

I cried for several more minutes. "He asked if I would come to the Midtown office tomorrow so we can plan out a strategy. I told him that would be all right—but look at me now."

Christina placed my hands on her stomach.

I said, "I do not know how I will be able to assist him, but he needs me."

Christina hugged me. "You will be all right. He will understand."

"He is a very caring man and will certainly be patient with me if he needs to be."

Christina nodded and said, "Yes, I am sure he will be."

I took another bite of my toast and a sip of tea. "He requested my presence tomorrow morning. Do you think I can handle it? I still feel so upset and confused."

"John, he needs you—or else he would not have asked. You may just want to give it a chance and see what happens. There may be a few people there—or at the very least just him."

I replied, "You mean there might be other people?"

"I don't know. What did he say when you spoke to him?"

"It sounded like it would just be the two of us."

"Okay, then, you have your answer. You can take the 8:05—that should get you there in plenty of time. We can check the train schedule together."

"Do you think the trains will be running tomorrow?"

"We can check the schedule and see. If they are not, you can always call him and reschedule."

"I guess they will probably go as far as Grand Central, but there may be some rerouting for the subway system in the downtown area."

"Just take it one thing at a time. We will get through this together. Why don't you finish your breakfast and then we can call Mother and tell her our news?"

"Christina, can you check the schedule and see if the trains are running today?"

"Why? Where are you going?"

"If they are running today, they will be running tomorrow as well."

"John, remember, one thing at a time. I had a muffin earlier this morning, but I am hungry. Remember, I am now eating for two."

I smiled and finished eating my breakfast and drinking my tea.

Christina finished scrambling her eggs and brought them over to the kitchen table. She sat down and began to eat. She reached under the table and placed her hand on my inner thigh. "I can think of other things we can do after I finish my eggs."

"I thought you wanted to call your mother? We also have to check the train schedule," I said.

"Mother can wait a while. There is no rush."

I stood up, closed my robe, lifted Christina from her seat, and carried her into the bedroom.

CHAPTER TWELVE

MOTHER

Gina was a widow. Her husband had died several years ago of a massive heart attack. He had worked as a supervisor at a large insurance company in New York City. He had invested wisely, and his life insurance policies left his wife financially comfortable. Gina lived in a large house near the seashore. She loved the water and the Milford area.

Gina was a friendly and gregarious woman who had many close friends. She had retired from the public school system after teaching English for more than thirty years. Her days were filled with baking, crafts, and socializing with friends. She loved her daughter, but they did not always see eye to eye. Gina and Christina were alike in many ways and usually tried to convince the other of their point of view.

They spoke daily, and Gina loved me. I was the son she never had. I was sensitive to her needs and generous with my attention. I felt very close to her and enjoyed our interactions.

At noon, Christina and I emerged from the bedroom. We walked into the family room and sat down. I decided to wait several hours before calling Metro-North. I turned to Christina and asked, "How do you think we should proceed with Mother?"

"I thought we could call her and tell her the good news."

"Don't you think that is a little too impersonal?" I asked.

"What idea do you have?"

"Why not call her and tell her we would like to drop by to speak to her?"

Christina looked up at me and raised her eyebrows. "You want to drive over there?"

"Yeah, I would like to see the expression on her face."

"All right then. Let's call her," Christina replied.

Christina walked over to the telephone and called Gina. "We are doing fine. Are you going to be home? We will be out doing some errands and wanted to drop by for a while. No, really, everything is fine. That will be great. See you in about an hour."

Christina gathered up the dry cleaning and headed to the car.

I opened my attaché case and picked up the scarf.

Christina went to the garage.

"Christina, there are some papers in the inside pocket of my suit jacket that I need. It is a good thing I remembered them," I said. I went to the garage and removed the papers from my suit jacket. "I will just be a minute." I ran back into the house and placed the papers inside my attaché case.

The Maple Tree Dry Cleaners was several miles away from our house. As we drove up to the building, Christina said, "Let me go in. I will just be a few minutes." She opened her door and reached in the back for the bag of clothes. Christina had suggested not bringing in my soiled clothes from the prior day.

I sat in the car and observed the people walking by. I remembered when Christina and I used to take walks down by the seashore. That was one of my favorite things to do. Hand in hand, we would pick up an occasional shell or take off our shoes and socks and run through the water together. I smiled.

There was another time when we built a sandcastle, and I declared that I was the king of the fortress. Christina made a crown out of seaweed and placed it on my head.

I was deep in thought and did not see Christina return to the car. She opened the door and startled me. As she entered, she had a grin on her face. "You will never guess who I just ran into. It was Richard and his wife. They asked us to drop by next weekend. I told her I had to look at the calendar and would let her know. What do you think?"

I said, "I don't know. I will have to see how I am at that time."

Christina appeared annoyed and said, "What do you mean?"

I was feeling anxious. "That is down the pike a bit—and I don't know how I will feel."

Christina said, "Think positive, John. It is good for you to get out and be with other people."

I said, "I know, but what if—"

"John, there will always be a what-if. I believe the best thing you can do is move on with your life."

I felt pressured and backed into a corner. "But you don't understand."

"Understand what? We should put our lives on hold for the possibility that you may not feel right?"

"What about me?"

"I like being with you as well as other people. We will drive each other nuts being confined to the house indefinitely."

"I am not saying that."

"What are you saying? Yesterday, you indicated that you were hoping Scott would call so we could get together. What are we going to say to him when he calls?"

"That's different," I said

"What are you saying?" Christina said.

"He understands what happened."

"John, I think most people who have watched television in the past few days have a clue about what happened."

"I am sorry if I am upsetting you."

"You are not upsetting me. I am just frustrated. I will tell Richard and Shirley that we have tentative plans, but I will try to change them and will let them know in a few days."

"You don't have to lie."

Christina said, "I am not lying. We do have plans. You and I may be in the shower together." She laughed.

"That sounds good to me. I am usually ready, willing, and able."

"I know what you like—and I am always willing to please," Christina replied.

The drive to Milford took about ten minutes. As we drove by the water, I could feel my whole body relaxing. I opened the window and took a deep breath. "This is heaven."

Christina smiled and gave me a kiss on the cheek.

I noticed that the white picket fence needed some fresh paint. "Christina, it looks like I have a project for the spring."

"That would be nice. I am sure Mom will appreciate it."

Before we could ring the doorbell, Gina opened the door. "You guys, what's the story? Is everything all right?" She looked at me and smiled.

"Mom, your fence needs painting. I thought I should come over and tell you in person."

"Oh, John. I can tell by your face that it is something more than that."

"Gee, Mom. I can't keep anything away from you. You are as sly as a fox."

"Let's go into the parlor and sit down," she said.

"Sounds good to us," I said.

We walked into the room and sat down on the plush, feather-filled chairs.

I said, "These chairs are so comfortable. Just give me a few minutes and some relaxing music, and I will fall asleep."

"That is no threat to me. Anytime," Gina replied.

"In about nine months, you are going to be a grandmother," Christina said.

Gina clutched her hands to her chest. "Congratulations. I am so thrilled. When did you find out?"

"Yesterday. I took the home pregnancy test. It was positive, and I have been suffering from morning sickness."

"That's my boy, John."

"How about me?" Christina said sarcastically. "I think I had something to do with this too."

"But of course, dear. You are the best—and what beautiful children you will make. Have you called the doctor?"

"No, Mom. You were the first stop. After the dirty laundry that is."

"Thanks, Christina. You know how to make your mother feel wanted."

"You will always be the greatest mother-in-law in the world as far as I am concerned," I said.

"Flattery will get you far in life," Gina said with a smile.

"It wasn't meant that way. It was the truth." I walked over to Gina and gave her a big hug and kiss. She was beaming and appeared elated by the news.

Christina stood up. "Okay, is everyone ready for a group hug?"

They all embraced and laughed.

"Let me make you sandwiches," Gina said.

"We are hungry, but we thought we would take a walk on the beach. Perhaps when we return. We also wanted to call the doctor to set up an appointment," Christina said.

"Can't you call him from here?"

"Mom, I don't have my calendar."

"I will be just a few minutes." Gina hurried into the kitchen.

"Mom, really, we want to go for a walk. We will be back soon, and then we can have a sandwich and some of your famous hot chocolate with marshmallows."

"Okay, children. Go enjoy yourselves. I will wait for you here."

Christina and I left the house. We were excited and looking forward to walking down to the beach. It reminded us of one of our first dates.

It was a sun-filled day without a cloud in the sky. The sea breezes made it seem a little cooler. Christina buttoned up her jacket. I asked if she was cold and put my arm around her. It felt good to be so close to her. She gave me a kiss on the cheek.

We walked hand in hand along a street that faced the water. A dog was barking in the distance. Garbage cans were lined up down the street like soldiers standing at attention. Each bungalow was different from the others and had been built before World War II for summer fun and entertainment. They were renovated to house families for the entire year. As they approached the beach, the aroma of the sea filled the air. I took a deep breath. "That smells so good. I really understand why you fell in love with this place."

As we approached the end of the street, we removed our shoes and continued down the sandy pathway to the beach.

It was the time of the day when few people frequented the beach. A few people were jogging or walking their dogs on the private stretch of white sand and rocks. A tanker heading toward New Haven Harbor, and several red and yellow buoys bobbed up and down to the sea's melodic rhythm. A few seagulls flew overhead, and others were perched on the rocks of the jetty.

"It is so good to be here. It makes me feel so relaxed," I said.

"I know how you feel, John."

"It is even better now that you are at my side." I reached over and kissed Christina.

Christina smiled, pulled me toward her, and kissed me on the lips.

I picked her up and swirled her in the air.

We laughed.

"Please put me down. I am getting dizzy," Christina said.

I stopped for a moment and said, "I'm sorry. I did not realize it—especially for a woman in your condition."

Christina smiled.

We walked onto the jetty, and Christina grabbed my hand. We stood at the end of the rocks, and Christina held my hand tightly and pulled me closer.

I turned and kissed her.

She looked up at me and said, "I remember coming here with my father when I was younger. I felt like we were marching into the sea. I was always afraid I would slip into the water—and he would have to rescue me."

"You better stay close to me then. I don't want to have to jump into the water." I jokingly nudged her toward the water.

"John, don't get any ideas," she said.

We embraced and kissed. I felt the warmth of her body next to mine. The softness of her lips and her scent excited me.

She looked into my eyes and said, "I love you."

I pulled her closer and kissed her again. I wanted to make love to her on the beach. We walked back to the sand and continued walking down the beach. I felt so alive.

I was feeling more and more relaxed. "You know, Christina, I am very conflicted about tomorrow. I am concerned about going into New York City again. It was so difficult for me yesterday. It was like a bad dream. I just wanted to wake up and be with you at home."

"I know, sweetheart. It must have been dreadful being there. Watching it on the television was bad enough." Christina replied.

"I never thought I would make it home. I was so frightened, and now I am standing here with you. It almost doesn't make sense. In some ways, I feel guilty that I am here."

Christina looked into my eyes and said, "You are here for a reason that only some higher power knows. It really is a miracle that you were spared. There is no logic to it. You may never know the real reason why. You need to be thankful for what you have and not think about what you could have done. There is no way you could have helped your work associates. They were placed in a most unfortunate situation. You cannot turn back the clock. It is what it is. You must move on and give back the gifts you have as a person. I love you, and soon enough, you will have a son or daughter in your life as well."

I held her close and said, "You just do not know how it feels. It is like a part of me has gone. I feel so empty and alone. I know you are there and love me, but I am lost in a never-ending sea of emotion." I looked out at the water.

"John, it will take time—just as it did in the past."

I stared at whitecaps and then turned back to her. "I realize that up here," he pointed to his head, "but in here," he pointed to his heart, "it just doesn't feel right. They are disconnected."

Christina stood in silence and waited.

"I know it will take time, but you know me. I am impatient, and I feel almost a total sense of lack of control. That is a feeling I am not familiar with having. Christina, I promise I will work on it. I am so sorry that I yelled at you last evening. I was so looking forward to seeing and being with you, and then I lost it."

"It is okay, John. Things do take a while. I realize that, but I am and will be patient."

"That is why I love you, Christina." I pulled her close and gave her a kiss.

"We should be heading back. Mom will send out the National Guard to find us."

We walked hand in hand back to the house. When we arrived at her gate, I unlatched it and Christina led the way into the house.

"Your mother was really surprised," I said.

"Yes, she was. You were right. Telling her in person was the correct thing to do."

"I knew she would be ecstatic. It is her first grandchild from her favorite daughter." I placed my hand on her shoulder.

"John, I am her *only* daughter."

"She loves you nevertheless. Take it as a compliment."

From the kitchen, Gina said, "Your lunch is ready."

Christina and I walked into the kitchen. It was a huge country kitchen that had been updated several times. Gina had it decorated to perfection with granite countertops, stainless steel appliances, white wooden cabinets, and a wooden floor. There were bar stools around a granite island. The double sink was below a window that overlooked the backyard, which was filled with hundreds of perennials. The kitchen table was next to a large family room with a wood fireplace. A large bay window had a view of the beautiful garden in the backyard. The table was set with three dishes, and each had a sandwich, chips, and pear wedges. There was also hot chocolate with marshmallows.

Christina indicated that she was hungry and was looking forward to lunch.

"Mom, I didn't realize you were preparing such a big lunch for us," I said in jest.

"Oh, sit down, funny man, and eat your sandwich and drink your hot chocolate before it gets cold."

"Yes, Mom!"

Christina and I were famished and quickly devoured our lunch.

When we finished, I said, "We hate to eat and run, but we have a lot to do, Mom."

"No problem. Go and enjoy. John, I am glad to see that you are doing okay."

"Thanks for lunch, Mom. We will call you later," I said.

CHAPTER THIRTEEN

GRAND CENTRAL STATION

I had a restless night and was tossing and turning. I had difficulty falling asleep because I kept on thinking about the meeting with my boss. I was going over so many questions in my mind. *What if he wants me to do something I cannot do? Will he expect me to call the families of the deceased? What if he wants me to plan a new program? Will I be able to think clearly? How will I get to the office? What if the trains are not running on time?*

I was obsessing about the next day and knew it, but could not do anything about it. I finally dozed off at two o'clock. I was able to sleep until the alarm went off at six. I turned to the clock and shut off the loud, piercing sound. *I want to remain in bed with Christina, but I had made a commitment to be in New York City. What is the day going to be like for me?*

On my way to the bathroom, I hit my leg on the side of the bed. "Oh shit," I cried out as I rubbed my leg. After my shower, I shaved and returned to the bedroom to dress. I decided to wear a suit and tie in case there were other people in the meeting. Although I was not feeling my best, I wanted to appear that way.

Christina was fully dressed and in the kitchen. I was surprised to see her. She apparently had been up for a while. Before I could speak, she informed me that she was driving me to the train station. In addition, she had already checked the train schedule, and it was going to be fifteen minutes late. She thought I should take the 7:45 instead of the 8:05. As she poured tea into a thermos and placed an egg-and-cheese sandwich in a brown paper bag, Christina informed that there was no time to waste. She told me to take my breakfast with me.

As I began to speak, she interrupted me and said that I should not even think about it because it was settled. She was driving me to the station. We lived ten minutes from the station, and she would have no problem picking me up later in the day.

When Christina made up her mind, it was final. There was no changing it. I grabbed my sandwich and tea and headed out to the car.

"John, have a good day. Expect the best. No negative thinking. It will get you into trouble. Right?"

"Yes, dear," I said sarcastically.

"That was not very convincing," Christina said.

"Yes, my honey bear," I jokingly said.

"That's better."

"John, you forgot your attaché case."

"I do not need it."

When I arrived at the station, a number of people were waiting on the platform.

"John, have a good day." Christina reached over and gave me a kiss.

"Thanks for being you." I kissed her warm, moist lips. "See you later."

I climbed up the stairs to the platform. The mood seemed very mellow. I wondered what these people had been doing two days ago. *I can't do this. I need to think about more important things. This is going to be the first day I am back to New York City.* I felt a surge of uneasiness. My face was flushed, and I had difficulty breathing. I took a deep breath and looked out to the horizon. I thought about being at the beach and hugging Christina. I started to feel better. I began to think about my boss. *How difficult is it going to be for him today? What will happen when I get to New York City?* The train pulled into the station, and I quickly found a seat. The blower was on, and warm air was being circulated throughout the car.

I was becoming more and more unsettled. I was on the verge of an anxiety attack.

An attractive redhead walked over and sat down next to me. She nodded and smiled.

I said, "It is always so dreadfully hot in these trains. You would think they would be able to regulate the heat more effectively."

"I know what you mean," she said as she took off her coat. She was wearing a blue suit with a sheer white blouse.

I removed my suit jacket and loosened my tie.

"Where are you off to today?" she asked.

"Midtown—and you?"

"I have business on Fifth Avenue. Let me introduce myself I am Katherine Warner." She held out her hand.

I shook her hand. "I am John Sable."

"Glad to meet you. I did not know what to expect today with the rail system. I had a horrible time getting home the other day. It took me six hours, and I was exhausted."

"I know what you mean. I had a hard time as well."

"What do you do in the city?" she asked.

I was feeling more relaxed. My uneasiness was more manageable, and the anxious feelings I was experiencing dissipated. This woman was either very friendly or was flirting with me. It had been a while since I was in that type of situation, and I was feeling uncomfortable. She was very appealing. I was becoming aroused, but I felt a sense of guilt. *What should I do? Perhaps I should excuse myself and move to another seat. If I am reading her incorrectly, she will feel insulted or hurt. Maybe my understanding of the situation is wrong or prompted by my own feelings. I am interested in how it is going to play out.* I said, "I work at an insurance company."

"That is interesting. I am in advertising. We represent several insurance companies."

She moved closer and stood up. "Do you mind if I reach over you and hang my coat on that hook?"

"No, not at all."

Katherine reached over me and rubbed against my leg.

I smelled her perfume and glanced at her nearly perfect body. I took a deep breath, and my face felt flushed.

She looked down at me and smiled. She sat down and crossed her legs, exposing her laced-trimmed slip. She quickly adjusted her skirt.

My suit jacket was serving as a cover on my lap. I wanted to hang it up, but I was embarrassed. I was aroused, and removing my coat would expose my excitement. I was really feeling frazzled.

"John, aren't you warm with the coat on your lap? Would you like me to hang it up for you?"

All I could think about was my current state. *Down, boy, down. What do other men do in situations like this?* I felt my face turning redder, and I began to perspire. "No, thank you. I am comfortable."

"John, are you sure? You appear hot."

"No thanks. I think I will just sit here and eat the sandwich my wife prepared for me. Would you like to share it with me?"

"I already had breakfast, but thank you for asking." She smiled again.

I thought eating would give me ample time to withdraw from the conversation. I unwrapped the sandwich and took a bite. I was hungry, and the eggs and cheese were cooked just the way I liked them. I opened my thermos and took a sip of tea. I glanced out the window. The train was pulling into the Stamford station. I would soon be in New York City. Once again, I was becoming distraught.

Katherine said, "Were you affected by that horrific event a couple of days ago?"

I felt my stomach tighten. *Just what I need someone to say,* I thought. I looked at her and said, "I am sorry, but that is something I would prefer not to talk about at this time. It is too painful for me."

The train pulled into the Stamford station, and there was an announcement.

Someone yelled, "Quiet!"

The conductor relayed information about transfers at the station, and he mentioned that there would be a slight delay before heading to 125th Street.

I wondered if I would be late for my meeting. I started to worry, but when I looked at my watch, I realized I still had plenty of time and calmed down. I took another sip of tea.

When the conductor finished speaking, Katherine looked into my eyes and said, "I am sorry. I would not have said anything if I knew it would upset you. Please excuse me."

"Ah, that is all right. I apologize if I was a little harsh, but it was a very difficult day for me. I have a lot of feelings that I have not resolved yet."

"John, please know I would never have asked if I had known."

"There is no way you would have known. It is not your fault."

"Tell me about your wife. She appears to make a good sandwich."

"Is there a Mr. Warner in your life?" I said.

"Of course. He is doctor, and we have three children—and you?"

"Not yet. We just celebrated our first anniversary on 9/11."

"That was bittersweet."

"In spite of what might have happened, be sure you take advantage and enjoy this time in your life." Katherine placed her hand on my jacket.

"I am working on it. It is not easy." I thought, *Please remove your hand—or it is going to lift off my lap.*

Katherine smiled. "I know, but you appear to be a physically strong and healthy man. Go with it, man." She lifted her hand from my coat.

When the train began to leave the station, I took another deep breath and sighed.

"Katherine, thank you for your words of encouragement."

"No problem. By the way, John, where do you live?"

"We live in Orange. How about you?"

"My husband and I live in Milford. I guess we are neighbors."

"Where is his practice?"

"He is a family physician, and his office is in New Haven. He is a wonderful doctor and is great with babies. You may want to look him up in the future."

"Thanks, Katherine. I will keep that in mind."

"It is getting warm in here. I think I will take you up on your offer about my jacket."

Katherine reached out, and I handed her my coat. I crinkled up the paper from my sandwich and placed it in the brown paper bag as Katherine reached over me. The train stopped short, and she fell onto my lap. She placed her warm hand on my thigh to regain her balance and moved back into her seat. My coat landed on the floor.

We both laughed.

I bent over and picked up my coat. I said, "Are you all right?"

"Yes, I am fine." She stood up.

The train started to move.

"Don't be silly. Please sit down. I got it." I hung my suit jacket on the hook, but it protruded into the seat. I had to move closer to Katherine. As I moved, my leg brushed against her. I quickly jerked it back and said, "Excuse me."

"That is all right. There is little space in these seats."

I was embarrassed and continued to drink my tea.

Katherine looked at me and said, "We will be at our destination soon, John. Be sure you remember what I said: 'It isn't what is there—it is what you make it out to be.' Let your mind take you in positive directions—and don't be weighed down by the detail and clutter."

"Thank you for your kind words, Katherine. I really need them and appreciate it."

"Don't mention it. You are a very nice guy. I enjoyed speaking to you this morning."

I looked out of the window and saw the sign for 125th Street. "We are pulling into the station. Just one more to go!"

Katherine smiled.

The train came to a screeching stop. The doors opened, and a number of people exited. Several people entered the train. The cool air filled the cars, and it felt refreshing.

The doors quickly closed, and the train was on its way to Grand Central Station.

I looked at my watch. I would be a half an hour early. It was a beautiful day, and I decided to walk to the office in Midtown. It would only take me twenty minutes. The fresh air would do me good. I would be able to clear my head and try to prepare myself for the meeting with my boss. The train was traveling through a tunnel. I stood up, reached for my jacket, and put it on. I handed Katherine her coat and sat down.

"Thank you, John. I guess that is it. Be sure to have a pleasant day."

"You too, Katherine, and thanks again for speaking with me today.

It really helped me—more than I can tell. I appreciate your kindness and sensitivity."

"John, there is no need to thank me. You are a special person, and the world needs more men like you. Hang in there."

The train stopped, and we walked onto the platform. As we separated in the sea of people, Katherine waved goodbye.

In the massive rotunda, I could hear the echoing of voices. I looked at the clock that marked the center of the room and the information booth. I had twenty minutes to walk to my office. There were several army men in the terminal. I had a troubling feeling. I began to think about Christina and decided to call her. To my amazement, there was service.

The cell phone rang several times. "Hi, Christina. Where were you?"

"In the bathroom. How are you doing, John?"

"It's been rough. It took me a while to settle down. My mind is so active, and I could not stop thinking about my previous experiences here and on the train."

"I can imagine, John," Christina said. "How are things now?"

"Somewhat better. I met this amazing woman on the train. She is from Milford. Her husband is a doctor in New Haven. She spoke very highly of him. They have three children."

"It seems as though you know her whole history."

"Yeah, she said you make the best sandwiches."

"Did you offer her some?"

A horn and siren went off.

"Where are you, John?"

"I am walking to the office. I had twenty minutes, and I thought the exercise and fresh air would do me good."

"You are probably right."

"Did you call the doctor, Christina?"

"I sure did. We have an appointment for tomorrow morning."

"That is great. I can't wait," I said.

"Me too."

"How was your morning after I left for work?"

"It was productive. I called the doctor's office, and I spoke to work and Mother. I also straightened up the house and did two loads of wash."

"You must be tired," I said.

"Not really. I paced myself, and I will be sitting down soon and watching some of my favorite shows on television. You know how much I enjoy the soaps. John, you are sounding better."

"Yes, I was fortunate to meet someone this morning. It took my mind off myself."

"You are probably right."

"Christina, I need to go. The office is just a block away."

"Good luck. Give me a call when you finish your meeting."

CHAPTER FOURTEEN
THE MEETING

I was surprised by the amount of activity on the street. There was traffic and the usual car horns and sirens. I looked across the street, and the deli had a long line of people waiting to be served.

I slowly approached the office building. It was a massive stone-and-steel structure with large glass windows. People were passing me, and I heard the rhythmic tapping of a cane behind me. I felt a wave of uneasiness and apprehension. I took a deep breath and entered the building.

The doorman was dressed in a blue-and-gray uniform and a gray cap. He greeted me with the customary nod and smiled.

I approached the elevators and the floors of each of the eight elevators were lit up. The second elevator appeared to be heading to the lobby, and I walked over to it. Several people followed me. I pushed the eighteenth floor and had a flashback to the last time I was in an elevator. My hand shook. Thank heavens it left quickly. I stepped aside to allow others to join me in the elevator. I thought about what Katherine had said and focused on the people in the elevator.

I recognized one of the men, but I could not remember his name. We did not make eye contact because there were several people between us. I felt closed in, but I knew it would only be for a short time. When the elevator reached the eighteenth floor I walked down the hallway to the office. As I opened the door I said, "Well, this is it."

I walked over to the reception area and identified myself.

A woman at the desk recognized me and smiled. She motioned for me to go right in. "Mr. Lawson is expecting you." The other woman appeared tired and unfocused. She was staring out the window.

I walked over to Mr. Lawson's office and was greeted by his secretary. "Go right in."

I opened the wooden doors, and my boss was at his desk. He stood up as I walked into the office. It was a large room with several floor-to-ceiling windows that overlooked the city. The carpeting was dark blue, and shelves lined the walls. Mr. Lawson's mahogany desk was really organized. Each piece of paper was meticulously placed. "John, please join me." He reached out and offered me a handshake.

I walked closer and shook his hand. I was nervous, but I tried my best to seem relaxed.

"Would you like something to drink?" Mr. Lawson asked.

"No thank you, Mr. Lawson."

He looked at me and smiled. "John, after all this time, you can call me Todd."

"Yes, sir."

"Enough with the formality, John, please."

I looked at my boss and thought, *He certainly doesn't look like a man who just lost several hundred employees two days ago. I wonder how he does it.*

"Now, John, you know that I am not one for small talk. I like to cut through all of the bullshit. How are you doing?"

I felt anxious and tense and was beginning to perspire. I felt self-conscious and was concerned and embarrassed. I looked at Todd and said, "It has been very difficult for me. I wish I would have been able to do more."

Mr. Lawson gazed into my eyes and said, "What do you mean?"

My eyes welled up with tears. "If I had the opportunity, I might have been able to rescue some of our people." I took a deep breath, exhaled, and moved my hands to my lap.

"John, that is very courageous of you, but you don't have a clear understanding of the gravity of the situation." Todd placed his hand on my shoulder. "When the plane hit, the people did not have any time to exit. They died instantly. It was a most ill-fated situation." Todd glanced out of the windows and shook his head.

He looked distraught.

Todd sat back down. "I myself cannot believe the Twin Towers do not exist anymore. It breaks my heart." He raised his hand to his chest. "So many of our workers perished in such a thoughtless act. We all feel some sense of loss, but we each handle it differently. I am grateful that you had the presence of mind and were able to travel here today. This is a difficult situation, and it will take a long time to recover from it."

"Thank you for keeping me in the loop, Todd," I said.

"You are a fine person and an excellent employee. You belong here."

"I appreciate that."

Todd walked over to one of the wall units and picked up a folder. "I prepared a list of things we have implemented in the last two days and what we plan on doing in the future. It has been a long two days. First of all, we are aware of who survived the incident. There are six of you. Three were at meetings out of the office, and three of you were late for work. The human resources department has contacted the families of those who died. In time, they will be provided a modified severance package. A group of individuals have been collecting donations, and a fund has been set up to assist the families who lost loved ones. The employees at our other offices will be picking up the slack until we can hire and train new recruits. We were fortunate to have an off-site backup system, and our records are intact. This information is part of phase one. There are other phases in the works."

"Yes, I see, Todd."

"Now, John, you are probably wondering where you fit into all of this."

I looked up at Todd and said, "Yes, I am."

"John, you will be heading up a team of people who will train the new recruits. However, there are a number of things that need to be accomplished first. I do not want to overwhelm you. Not everyone is ready to move forward yet. I am aware of the emotional distress that many feel. This is not an easy time for any of us. I do not want to place you in a situation you cannot handle. We have a support team that I want you to contact immediately."

I asked, "What do you mean by a support team?"

"We need to determine what effect this trauma has had on you. We are asking you to meet with a counselor who is trained in situations like this. These people are specifically prepared to deal with life-threatening situations and trauma."

"But, sir, I am handling it on my own," I said firmly.

"You *think* you are. I am glad you are, but I would like a professional to take a look at you. Whatever you say to him will be held in the strictest of confidence. No one here thinks you are mentally disturbed. On the contrary, we know you are sound. Otherwise, you would not be sitting across from me this morning. I am sorry, but you need to take advantage of this service. We have invested a lot of time and effort in you, and you are one of our best workers. I hope you will agree to my offer. Why don't you sleep on it and give me a call in the morning?"

I was in a daze and did not know how to respond. It was the second time someone had recommended counseling to me.

"John, you are doing what I often do. You are overthinking the situation, right?"

"Yes. How did you know?"

"Because we are alike, and it is what we do. Our brains get in the way all of the time. We are detail-oriented men. If we could roll back the clock and look at your desk, it would appear very much like mine, right?"

"Yes."

"Please think it over, do what I requested, and give me a call in the morning. Now—just for clarification—it would be like a regular workday. You would go to the human resources department and meet with the counselor. They will determine the length of time. When you complete the assignment for the day, you will return home. Your salary and benefits will remain the same. Got it?"

"Yes."

"Then I will speak to you tomorrow."

"Yes."

"Thank you again for coming in today. I appreciate everything you have already done for the company, and I anticipate that we will be spending more time together in the future."

"Thank you for the confidence you place in me." I reached out to shake his hand.

Todd shook my hand, nodded, and opened the door.

I left his office and felt overwhelmed by the experience. I had not been aware that I was so valued by the company. I had underestimated my worth to the company. I thought about Todd's recommendation while I waited for the elevator. Todd had made it pretty clear. If I was going to continue working at the company, I would need to contact the human resources department.

I evidently had no choice. I was uneasy about being told what to do, but I had to do it or look for another job. If I don't want to leave the company, I must comply.

I left the building and called Christina. Where the World Trade Center used to be, smoke was rising to the sky. I looked down to the pavement and began walking back to Grand Central.

"Hello, sweetheart," Christina said.

"Do you say that to every gentleman who calls you?" John said.

"No, silly. I just assumed it was you. If it were a telemarketer, he would think I was a little friendly. How did your meeting go?"

"There is a lot to talk about. He offered me my job with certain conditions."

"Do you want to share those with me?"

"It was a difficult meeting. We discussed my reaction to the events of the past couple days. At times, my mind was a blur, but Todd kept on redirecting the conversation to the company and the plan he has been working on. At first, I was unclear why he had asked me to the office, but he explained how he felt about me as an employee."

"John, what do you mean?"

"It seems that the company values me as a member of their staff, but they want to be sure that I can handle the next phase of the work plan. He is requesting that I become involved with the human resources department's counseling program."

"How do you feel about his proposal, John?"

A loud siren wailed in the distance.

I paused for a moment and then said, "I have to think about it. He gave me until the morning. I can't fathom sharing my inner thoughts and feelings with a stranger, but I need this job."

"John, you can always try it and see what happens."

"I guess so, but what if I get worse?"

"You can discuss your apprehension and fears with the counselor and see what he has to say. If you still feel uncomfortable, you can change your mind. You have nothing to lose."

"I guess you are right," I said. "I will see you in a few hours. I am almost at Grand Central. I guess I have a lot to think about."

I entered the train terminal and headed down the corridor. It was early in the afternoon, and there was a noticeable absence of people. I looked up at the display panel of the train schedules and saw that the next train was departing to New Haven in fifteen minutes. I decided to use the lower-level bathroom. I walked downstairs and headed to the restroom. I approached the rows of tables. There were several people eating and drinking. I looked over to one of the food stands and saw a delicious doughnut. I continued to the restroom. When I finished, I walked over to the counter and purchased the doughnut and a cup of tea. I walked over to the train and rested my head against the window. It had been a long morning. I was glad I had traveled to the city and had an opportunity to speak to Todd. I was exhausted and closed my eyes. I was soon in a deep sleep and began to dream about happier days with Christina.

We were honeymooning at a large hotel on Paradise Island in the Bahamas. We were in our hotel room.

"Christina, I am going to catch you."

"No, you are not." She ran into the other room.

"Oh, yes, I am." I chased her with a water gun.

Christina shot me in the face, ran into the bathroom, and slammed the door.

"Open this right now. I have a surprise for you."

"Blah, blah, blah," she said.

"You are going to get it one way or another."

"Not if you can't catch me."

"Oh, I will catch you." I knocked on the door.

"Quiet, John. You are going to wake up everyone in this place."

"Who are you kidding? It is only eleven o'clock."

"Some people go to bed early."

"Do you want to spend the rest of your honeymoon with the toilet?"

"You are a comedian, John. I will open the door if you promise to put your gun away."

"I would like to see your handsome face again. All right, I promise."

"Now you wouldn't be lying to your wife of twenty-six hours, would you?"

"Of course not," I said sarcastically.

"Here I come." She tried to open the door. The knob turned, but the latch did not disengage. "Oh no."

"What's the matter?"

"I think the door is jammed. Oh shit. It will not open. What should I do?"

"Let me think. Perhaps I can take off the hinges. Oh no!"

"What now?" Christina shouted.

"The hinges are inside the bathroom."

"What do you expect me to do? I have nothing in here but a roll of toilet paper."

"I need to call the front desk."

"John, not so fast. Remember, I don't have a stitch of clothing on. If you look at yourself, you are probably wearing what I am."

"You are right? I better put on some pants. Why don't you wrap a towel around yourself?"

Christina said, "May I remind you that I have no clothes on my body—nothing."

"So, wrap a towel around yourself."

"John, take a good look around you. The towels are in the outer bathroom. There is only toilet paper in here."

"I guess we have a dilemma. I still have to call the front desk. I will hand you a towel once they unjam the door. Don't worry."

"Easy for you to say."

I slipped on a pair of pants and a T-shirt and called the front desk. "Christina, they are sending someone right up."

"I hope they get here soon," Christina said.

Ten minutes later, there was knock at the door. I opened it, and two men entered the bridal suite and one of the men proceeded to the bathroom. The other man stood by the door.

"I see we have a problem with the door—and the little lady is inside," the man said with a smirk.

People were passing by the door and looking in to see what was happening.

"Do you think we should close the door?" I asked.

The repairman looked up at me and said, "No. It is hotel policy that we have to keep the door open while we are in the room."

Wonderful, John thought. *We have an audience, and I did not even put on underwear.*

While the repairman was evaluating the situation, people continued to congregate in the hallway.

I shrugged and said, "The bathroom door is jammed, and my wife is inside."

The repairman looked up and said, "This should be fixed in a few minutes. The same thing happened in 704 about a week ago."

I whispered, "We have one slight problem."

"What might that be?"

I said, "My wife is in there with no clothes on her body, and there are no towels."

The man said, "So, the missus is on the other side of the door without any clothing on?"

This piqued the people's interest in the hallway.

I realized the repairmen were not going to be discrete about the situation and decided to take matters into my own hands. I walked over to the door and closed it. I turned to the repairman and said, "I am renting this room and want privacy. You can go downstairs, report it to management, and have them call me." I walked over to the bathroom and picked up a towel.

At that moment, the doorjamb was repaired, and the men went to open the door.

I said, "Just a minute—I can handle this!"

The man let go of the handle and retreated.

I said, "Christina, I am handing you a towel." I opened the door a crack and threw the towel into the bathroom. I reached into my pocket, took out several dollars, and handed it to the man. "Thank you. I can handle it from here. Please close the door on your way out."

The train stopped short and woke me up. I was unsettled and confused, but I quickly realized I was on the train heading home. I thought about the dream and smiled. I looked out the window and noticed that we had just left the Bridgeport station. I would be in Milford in fifteen minutes. I stretched and reached out my arms. I had really needed that sleep. I was feeling invigorated and was looking forward to being home. The people around me were reading newspapers, working on laptops, or talking on their phones. I decided to drink my tea and eat the doughnut.

When I finished eating the doughnut, I called Christina and told her I would be at the station within ten minutes.

When the train arrived at the station, Christina was waiting with the others who were picking up passengers. It was a warm day, and the sun was shining brightly. Christina took a pair of sunglasses out of her pocketbook.

I was one of the first to exit.

Christina's face lit up, and her eyes sparkled.

I crumbled the bag and threw it into the garbage.

Christina turned her head toward me, and we kissed.

"I am so glad to see you," I said.

"I am too. I was looking forward to this moment all day. Tomorrow morning is our first appointment with the doctor."

"I know—and I can't wait. I think I will call Todd and tell him that I would like him to set up an appointment for me."

"That is great." Christina placed her hand on my inner thigh.

I gave her a kiss on the cheek.

"Meet anyone interesting on the train on your way home?" Christina asked with a smirk.

"Yes, there were these repairmen who were trying to open a jammed door of a bathroom of this couple on their honeymoon."

Christina laughed. "I guess you took a nap?"

"Yes."

When we arrived home, I excused myself to go to the bathroom. I entered the washroom next to the kitchen, and Christina headed for the bedroom. When I was finished washing my hands, I opened the door and called for Christina.

Christina shouted, "John, why don't you see if you can find me?"

"What do you mean?" I replied.

"I have a surprise for you."

In the bedroom, Christina was on the bed with her legs spread apart. She was beautiful and very appealing. I took off my suit jacket and tie. I began to unbutton my shirt, exposing my well-sculptured chest.

Christina smiled and gestured for me to approach her. I took off my shoes and dropped my pants to the floor. I jumped onto the bed. I shimmied my way up to Christina and gave her a kiss on her lips. "You are so beautiful. I love you." I began caressing her body, kissing her nipples through the transparent lingerie. I removed her panties and then kissed her. I felt for her clitoris. She was moist, and I placed my tongue inside of her.

"That is good," she cried out.

I placed myself on top of her.

She took her hand and directed me inside of her.

I groaned with delight. I felt my body shiver as her warm, moist fluids encircled my erect shaft. I continued to satisfy her.

"You have such a cute ass," she lovingly said. She held me tight.

I moved up and down, and with each thrust, I entered her deeper.

We moved together in perfect harmony.

I smothered her with kisses. I felt the vibrations within her as I let my mighty flow go.

We embraced in complete rapture and fell asleep in each other's arms.

CHAPTER FIFTEEN

THE DOCTOR'S VISIT

The sun began its ascent, and our bedroom was soon full of the bright rays shining through the windows. Christina and I greeted the morning with a kiss and then took showers and began our morning routines.

I called my boss to inform him of my decision.

The receptionist placed me on hold.

My heart began to pound.

"Todd Lawson here."

"Good morning, sir."

"Oh, it is you, John."

"Yes."

"I was expecting your call."

"Mr. Lawson, I have carefully thought about your proposition and decided to meet with the human resources department. Can you arrange an appointment for me? Any time after today will be fine."

"Yes, John—or should I call you Mr. Sable?" Todd said jokingly. "I will do just that and have my secretary call you to confirm the day and time."

"Thank you, sir. Have a nice day."

"You too—and my best to your wife."

"Thank you. Goodbye, sir."

I hung up the telephone as Christina walked into the kitchen. "I just spoke to Mr. Lawson."

"I thought I heard you speaking to someone. I believe it is the right decision."

I looked at Christina and said, "The office is going to call me later with a day and time."

"Great." She walked over and gave me a kiss on the cheek. She stated that she was proud of me.

I smiled. "Do you want to have breakfast here—or should we go out?"

"I think it would be best to stay here. The coffee shop can be very busy in the morning, and I am concerned about being on time for our appointment."

"Christina, why don't you sit down while I prepare something for you to eat," I said.

"That would be nice. Thank you."

I placed several eggs on the counter. One began to roll. I stopped it and placed them in a bowl. I took another bowl out of the cabinet, broke open several eggs, and scrambled them. I placed several slices of rye bread in the toaster and poured two cups of coffee. When the toast was ready, I buttered each piece and placed them on plates with the eggs. I then carried the plates and coffee to the table.

Christina smiled. "These eggs are delicious, and rye toast is my favorite."

As we finished breakfast, I looked at my watch.

Christina said, "John, we have plenty of time. Don't worry."

"Christina, why don't you get ready while I clean up?" I walked over to the answering machine and made sure it was on.

As we were driving to the doctor's office, I said, "Christina, I am excited and a little nervous. I do not know what to expect."

"I am glad you said something. I am feeling the same way," Christina added.

In the office, we gave our names to the receptionist.

Christina filled out a packet of information.

I looked up at Christina and apologized that I did know my parents' medical history.

"It's all right. We can only provide the information we know."

When we completed the forms, I brought the paperwork back to the receptionist.

Fifteen minutes later, a nurse called for us.

We followed the nurse to an examining room.

"You are next. The doctor will be right with you." She handed Christina a gown. "Please put this on with the opening in the back."

I thought, *Is he going to examine her from the rear?*

I sat down while Christina changed into the blue-and-white gown.

There was a knock at the door, and it swung open.

A short, stout man in white lab coat and white clogs introduced himself as Dr. Stern. He smiled and held out his hand. "You must be the Sables." Shaking each of our hands, he said, "I am so glad to meet you."

We were both put instantly at ease.

"Okay, let me explain what I will be doing." He walked over to the sink and washed his hands. "First, I am going to examine you, and then we will talk about my findings." He dried his hands and put on rubber gloves.

When he completed the examination, he said, "I have reviewed the paperwork and have performed the initial examination. Everything seems to be all right. How have you been feeling?"

"I am fine, but I have been experiencing some morning sickness," Christina replied.

"That is to be expected. Do you have any questions for me?"

Christina said, "My husband and I were wondering if we can continue having relations."

Dr. Stern said, "That is a common question. Most young couples are concerned about intercourse. You have nothing to worry about. The fetus is protected."

I said, "It will not hurt the baby?"

"No, I can assure you there is nothing to worry about. Sometimes, there is concern for women who are at high risk, but there is nothing that I can tell from your history or the examination that is the case. Is there anything else?"

"Yes," Christina said. "Do I need to be on a special diet?"

"Christina, you appear to be in good physical shape. I will be running some blood tests to check things out. My assistant will take a blood sample in a few minutes. We should have the results within a week. I will be writing you a prescription for vitamins. These will be a little stronger than what you can buy over the counter. Continue to eat a healthy diet. You know, plenty of fresh fruits and vegetables, grains and meat, chicken and fish. If there is anything to report from the blood tests, I will contact you. If you do not hear from me, assume everything is fine. Why don't I see you in another month? Please set something up with the receptionist. It was nice meeting you. I'm looking forward to treating you. Until later." Dr. Stern walked out of the room.

Christina dressed and waited for the nurse to return. "He seems very nice."

"I think so. He is very personable—don't you think?" I said.

The physician's assistant entered the room. "You must be the Sables. I am glad to meet you. I am Tom. This will only take a few minutes. Tom withdrew blood from Christina's arm and put two test tubes on the counter. He placed a Band-Aid on her arm. There we are. You are finished and can leave. See you next month."

I looked at Christina and asked, "Christina, would you like to stop for a treat?"

"Yes, let's stop at the coffee shop for lunch."

"We can then stop at Mother's house and share the results of the examination."

"That will be great."

When we arrived at the coffee shop, we were both starving. We ordered burgers, fries, and milkshakes. We spoke about plans for the baby and which room of the house would be the best. After apple pie and ice cream, we decided to go see Gina.

As we drove up to the house, Gina was planting bushes.

"Mom, I could have done that," I shouted.

"I know, John, but I like to keep busy."

Gina stopped what she was doing, stood up, and removed her gloves.

We discussed the doctor's appointment at the kitchen table and left.

As we passed the seaside, Christina reached over and gave me a kiss. "I am so happy."

I winked and said, "I am very much in love with you."

Christina smiled and placed her hand on her stomach.

CHAPTER SIXTEEN
HUMAN RESOURCES

Christina and I had a relaxing evening. We watched *Moving Violations* on television, and it was hilarious. We went to bed at ten o'clock.

I had some difficulty sleeping. I was thinking about my appointment and did not know what to expect. The only counseling I had received was with a guidance counselor in high school when I was applying to colleges. The process was long and tedious, and in my opinion, it was a waste of time. I had high marks, was on several sport teams, and scored high marks on the college entrance exams. Thinking about my family history, especially in regard to my parents, was upsetting to me. In fact, the application process had been more stressful than awaiting my acceptance letter from Yale University.

Now, because of circumstances beyond my control, I had to be examined by someone I had never met. What could that person possibly tell me that I didn't know already? I felt it was up to me to work through my own problems, conflicts, and concerns. I should take the responsibility to resolve any issues that existed. It was not a job for anyone else.

I was not looking forward to meeting with the human resources department, but I had made a commitment. I would need to follow through. On the train, I thought about the process. My job depended on it, and it was important to Christina. I would need to come to terms with that adventure in my life. Perhaps the counselor could assist me in some way, but I did not have a clue how that was going to happen.

A few rows in front of me, I saw the woman I had given money to on 9/11. We made eye contact, and I nodded. She smiled. I walked over to her. She was alone, and I sat down. "How did everything work out?" I asked.

"Just fine," the woman said. She appreciated my generosity. Her husband was doing well, and she was able to secure another job. Her sister-in-law knew someone who was looking for a day worker. She applied and was accepted. Today was the first day of her job.

"How are things with you?" She wanted to repay me and reached into her pocketbook.

"That is not necessary," I said. "That was the least I could do for you and your family. Please put away your money."

"No," she said. "It was fate that we saw each other again today. It would mean a lot to me if you would let me give you back the money."

"Okay, if you insist."

She opened her purse and handed me several bills. "What happened with your job?"

"I am still working in New York. In fact, I am heading there now."

"That is great. Take care of yourself—and may the Lord bless you."

"He already has blessed us." My eyes filled with tears. I looked down as I stood up. "You have a good day."

"Thank you."

The train arrived on time. I felt that it was a good sign. Perhaps it was going to be a good day. I took a brisk walk to the office. The streets were crowded with people. I noticed several yellow taxicabs and buses. The day appeared like any other one.

I rode the elevator to the seventeenth floor and walked down the corridor. I could smell the fresh paint that was recently applied to the walls.

The receptionist at the front desk said, "We've been expecting you. Let me walk you to Dr. Marks's office." She led me down a short hallway to the office and knocked on the door.

"Come in."

The office was much larger than I had expected. There was a modern desk by a window that faced downtown. Two chairs were in front of the desk. There was also a sitting area. Several floor-to-ceiling bookcases lined one wall, and diplomas and a painting were hung on another. Dr. Marks used indirect lighting. Several floor lamps were placed strategically around the room.

I stood at the open door.

"Please come in and join me. I am Dr. Marks, but you can call me Jay. Mr. Lawson told me to expect you. Sit down. Can I get you anything? How about a hot drink?"

"Tea would be nice."

"Lemon or cream?"

"Neither."

"Fine." He pushed the intercom. "Jeanette, can you bring us a tea and a coffee? Thanks.

"So, John, what brings you here?"

"Well, it seems to me that you already know the answer to that question."

The therapist looked at me and replied that it didn't matter what he thought. What were important were my impressions.

I thought, *Here we go with the first head game.* "I was told—maybe I should say that it was strongly suggested—that I consider the services you are offering in order to work through any issues I might be having in relation to 9/11."

"Oh, you think you are here because you were told to be here?" Dr. Marks said.

"Yes—and furthermore, I really wouldn't have volunteered to be here."

"Can you tell me where you were on 9/11? John, before you begin, let me be clear that whatever you might say will be held in the strictest of confidence. Do you understand?"

"Yes, but—"

"No, John. There are no exceptions unless you present a danger to yourself or others."

There was a knock at the door. The secretary brought in the hot beverages and quickly left the room.

I said, "Don't you need to let Mr. Lawson know what progress is being made?"

"No, he just will be told initially that you have begun the program. Whether you finish it or not is your business—not anyone else's."

I was feeling better about the process. I had thought Mr. Lawson would be given ongoing progress reports in order for me to continue my employment.

"So, John, where were you on 9/11?" Dr. Marks asked again.

"I was at home in Orange, Connecticut, with my wife. Christina was sleeping when I left for the train station. I was on time, but the train was running late. When I reached Grand Central Station, the train stopped for a while. It seemed like something was wrong, but I did not know what was happening."

"Something was wrong?" Dr. Marks asked.

"Yes, there were no lights except for the auxiliary ones, and the ventilation system was out. Then the conductor announced that the passengers on the train needed to exit, walking through the cars until they reached the first car. That door would lead them to the tracks, which ultimately would take them to the platform. I was directed to a secondary exit, and when I walked into the street, there was utter chaos. People were running in all directions away from the World Trade Center. They appeared in a state of shock and terror. They were yelling. It seemed to me that Tower One was on fire. When I looked up, there was thick smoke coming from the upper floors."

"And?"

"I assumed there was a fire. I did not know that a plane had crashed into the building. I tried to enter the building, but I was turned away. The police were not letting anyone enter the building other than police and firemen. I really wanted to enter the building."

"How were you feeling?"

"I was frustrated and angry."

"Angry?"

"Yes! I was fucking angry. I wanted to go into the building to see if I could be of some assistance. My friends were in that building. I felt that the police could have let me enter."

"John, you understand that the building was on fire and it was dangerous situation."

"How do you know that? You just assume that, right?" My eyes welled up with tears. "I felt it was my responsibility to do something, and I owed them that. After all, I was their supervisor."

"No, John, you did have a responsibility to them, but you did not owe them your life. Who did you see leaving the building?"

"People who were covered with soot and blood. Some had difficulty breathing. It was a horrific sight." I started to cry. "Why did this have to happen? We did not do anything wrong. They were good people and did not deserve to die." I held my hands to my face, and my body began to shake.

"You are right. There is no plausible explanation."

"I wanted to enlist in the army and kill each and every one of those sons of bitches. They are the ones who ought to die—not us. I was in a partial daze and continued down the street. There was ash and debris all over the place." I wiped my nose with my jacket sleeve.

Dr. Marks handed me a box of tissues.

"Then there were those thumping sounds."

"Thumping?"

"Yes, I saw them."

"What did you see?"

"There were people from the upper floors. They must have been above the floors that were burning, and there was no way out for them. They jumped. It was so fast. There was a thump and a slushing sound. Oh Lord, they jumped to their death. I saw and heard them. One landed only twenty-five feet away from me." I looked away from Dr. Marks and gazed out the window. Tears were rolling onto my shirt. I reached for a tissue and blew my nose.

"How often?"

"It happened several times. I cannot rid my mind of that scene. It was like a horror movie. When I dream about it, I feel so helpless."

Dr. Marks looked horrified.

"What could I have done?"

"As you see by your experience at the site, there was nothing that you could have done," Dr. Marks replied. "John, can you discuss the dream?"

"Do you really think it will be helpful?"

"Yes," Dr. Marks replied. "It would be useful."

I looked up to the ceiling. "When I arrived at my office, I walked into the conference room. They were about to start the meeting when someone pointed out the window at a jumbo jet."

"A jumbo jet?"

"Yes, it was heading right into the building. It looked like it was going to crash right into the building. I took cover."

"What did you do?"

"I sheltered myself under the table, and the plane crashed into the building. There was a loud explosion. When I looked up, there was a wall of flames. People were burning, and there were dead bodies all over the place. It was getting hotter and hotter. The floor was consumed with flames. I felt helpless. I could not do anything."

"Helpless?"

"I could not move, and the flames were getting closer to me. I started to yell for help, but nobody came to rescue me. I woke up, and Christina was cradling me. I wanted to do something. What could I have done?"

Dr. Marks said, "Unfortunately, nothing—other than praying for their souls."

"You are right," I replied. "I couldn't stop my mind from thinking about it. What should I do? How do others handle it?"

"You have taken the right step by contacting this office. Talking is a way of working through your feelings. This is how others deal with the issues. Your story is very compelling, and you are releasing a tremendous amount of emotion. I can feel your distress, and I empathize with you. It will take time, but you will get there."

"How can you determine how I am functioning if this is the first time I've met with you?"

"That is a good question. It is how you are relating the information that you are sharing. You are logical, coherent, and appropriate."

"Appropriate?" Tears were streaming down my face.

"John, it may be hard for you to believe, but that is an appropriate reaction to the trauma you experienced. In your state, you also managed to find your way home?"

"I walked for miles until I came to a bridge and crossed over the Hudson River. I met a man named Scott, and he was a lifesaver. At first, I did not particularly like him, but after several hours, I grew to like and respect him."

"What about him did you respect?"

"He just seemed to care and tried to provide me support. I also met other people along the way who were in need of assistance."

"What do you mean?"

"There was a woman who was frightened and scared. Her office was located near the Twin Towers. She was afraid to go home because she had no money for food for her children. She was supposed to be paid that day, and her office was closed. I believe it was demolished. I offered her some money."

"She probably appreciated the money."

I focused my attention to the window. "You will never believe this story. Today, on my way to the office, I ran into that woman on the train. We spoke for a while. She was able to secure new employment. I was so happy for her."

Dr. Marks looked at his watch and said, "John, our time is over for today. It would be desirable for us to meet and speak tomorrow at the same time."

I felt somewhat relieved. I felt a major burden had been lifted from my shoulders. I still had major concerns about the incident, but I was more willing to share my experience with the doctor. Dr. Marks was a good listener and understood me. I still had some doubt about the process, but I was willing to give it a chance.

I wiped a tear that had fallen to my cheek and agreed to Dr. Marks's suggestion.

"Good, let us meet again tomorrow." Dr. Marks handed me a folder.

I thumbed through the papers.

Dr. Marks said, "If possible, could you fill out these papers for tomorrow? It will help me better understand you in the context of your story."

I looked up at Dr. Marks and said, "Can't you just ask me the questions?"

Dr. Marks replied, "Filling out the papers is a good exercise and will help you think about the major milestones in your life. We will be able to speak about them when we meet again."

I left the office and walked to the elevator. I looked at the papers and shook my head. I was not happy, but I had no choice. The elevator doors opened, and it was packed.

Someone said, "Come on in. There is always room for one more." I hesitated and then walked into the crowded elevator.

As the doors shut, my body tensed up. I had a flashback to the subway and the night of 9/11. My heart began to beat faster, and my breathing became more labored. I was thankful that the elevator did not make any additional stops on its way to the ground floor. As the doors opened, I quickly walked to the street and took a deep breath. I was sweating, and the cool air felt good. I decided to call Christina.

"Hi, I am glad you're home. I needed to speak to you," I said.

"Is everything all right?" Christina said.

"Yes, now it is."

"What do you mean?" Christina asked.

"I left Dr. Marks's office and entered a crowded elevator. I had a panic attack."

"Do you know what caused it?"

"I had a flashback to the night of 9/11, standing in the subway car."

"Where are you now?" Christina asked.

"I am walking toward Grand Central."

"But are you okay?"

"Yes, it seemed to pass once I left the elevator and walked into the street."

"I am glad you are doing better."

"Christina, how was your day?"

"It was all right. We are busy at the office, so the day goes by quickly. What do you want for dinner?"

"I don't care. Surprise me," John said.

"I can't wait to see you, John."

I have been thinking about you and your session all day. John, have a good trip home. Did you grab something to eat for the train ride? You never know who you might meet."

I replied, "Very funny, Christina. No, I did not buy anything. I thought I would wait for dinner."

"Call me when you get close to the station. Speak to you then. I love you. Goodbye."

I entered Grand Central, walked into the rotunda, and looked at the monitor to see when the next train was leaving. I had seven minutes to get to the track. I moved quickly through the station. The train was filling up, but there was still plenty of room. I breathed a sigh of relief. I walked through several cars and sat down. I removed my suit jacket and hung it on the hook next to my window. There were several people seated near me. I smelled pepperoni, and it made me hungry.

I began filling out the paperwork. As the train pulled out of the station, I began to feel very tired. The melodic rocking of the train put me to sleep.

When I woke up, the train was pulling into the Bridgeport station. I had not made much progress with the paperwork. I called Christina and told her that I would be arriving in Milford in about ten to fifteen minutes.

Christina rushed me off the telephone so that she would be able to meet the train on time.

As the train approached the Milford station, I had a feeling of relief. When I spotted the car, I waved to Christina. I walked quickly to the car, opened the door, and gave Christina a kiss.

"That was a great appetizer. What is the main dish going to be?" Christina asked.

I placed my hand on her thigh and said, "Anything your heart desires."

I smiled and kissed her cheek.

"John, what do you have on your lap?"

"Dr. Marks gave me some papers to fill out. He told me that it would help with the treatment. I already started to fill them out, but I fell asleep. Hopefully, I will have better luck tonight. He wants me to have them ready for tomorrow."

"John, when we arrive home, why don't you freshen up while I finish making dinner? You can complete the paperwork."

I gave her a look of disgust.

"John, it will not be that bad. Just make believe you are applying for a new job—or filling out a college application."

"Exactly," I said in a sarcastic manner.

"John, you are overthinking the process. Just do it—and then we can have a treat."

"A treat? Are you trying to motivate me?"

Christina said, "I would call it more of an *enticement*."

The evening went by quickly, and I was looking forward to my next session. The next morning, I used the time on the train to review the paperwork.

"John, how was your evening?" Dr. Marks asked.

"Good."

"Did you fill out the paperwork?"

"Yes, it is in my pocket. I will get the papers for you." I handed them to him.

"John, let me take a few minutes to review the information ... you have good penmanship."

While Dr. Marks was busy, I looked around the office. It reminded me of a living room or study. The only thing missing was a fireplace. The light shined in through the drapes. The indirect lighting provided a soft, comfortable atmosphere. Several oil paintings of landscapes adorned the walls. A number of knickknacks were on the tables. I especially liked the puzzles and the jar of candy beside me. I picked up one of the hand puzzles and started to manipulate it.

"John, you were quite an athlete and the president of your class in high school. Can you tell me about it?"

I put down the puzzle and said, "I always seemed to excel in sports. When I was younger, my dad registered me to play baseball and soccer. I was placed on the travel team, and we won several tournaments.

When I was older, I joined the football team. My mother was not thrilled because of the possibility of injuries. However, my dad was a football player in high school and wanted me to play varsity. He eventually convinced my mom. It was a good thing because I earned a college scholarship. I played all four years. My high school team made it to the state finals. In high school, I was elected president of the class and voted the most likely to succeed."

"John, you have done just that. You are very well respected in the insurance field from what I understand. So, you were quite the leader."

"I never really looked at it that way. I really enjoyed what I did, and people seem to like me."

"Did you ever come into conflict with any situations?"

"There was a professor I had who did not like me very much. I do not know why, but he always seemed critical of my work. I had never experienced anything like that before, and it was a very difficult semester. I believe there was more to it."

"What do you mean?"

"He made me feel very uncomfortable."

"In what way?"

"The way he used to look at me. You know the feeling you get when a guy looks at you funny?"

"Funny?"

"Yeah, like he is looking you over. The way a woman might look at you."

"Oh?"

"I thought it best to ignore him—in case I was misreading the situation."

"Misreading?"

"Yeah, even speaking about it makes me feel uncomfortable. Men do not act in that way unless they are interested in you."

"Interested?"

"Like they want something more than a casual relationship. I once walked up to his desk and noticed class photos of several guys on his desk. The whole situation did not make me feel good. Looking back at what happened, I think he might have been gay and been attracted to me. I am not interested in that kind of relationship and never have been. It is all right if someone is gay, but this guy apparently had some difficulties handling his feelings toward me."

"Do you think his being in a position of authority made it more threatening to you?"

"Yes, I felt vulnerable. It is not a good feeling."

"Control is important to you."

"Yes, isn't it to everyone?"

"To some—but not everyone."

"What do you mean?"

"Some people like to have control, and some like to be controlled. You are a leader, and it is important for you to be in control. There have been two episodes in your life where you have felt upset and distraught. The first was when your parents died, and the other was 9/11."

I dropped my head and looked down.

"John, would you like to tell more about the circumstances surrounding your parents' death?"

I continued to look down. "I was home from graduate school at the time. I was sick with an upper respiratory infection. The doctor ordered an antibiotic. My parents were out for dinner at a friend's house. They decided to stop at the pharmacy and pick up my prescription. If I recall, it was raining. On their way home, someone ran a stop sign and plowed into their car. The medical examiner said they must have died instantly." My eyes began to fill with tears.

"John, how did you feel at the time?"

"Terrible." I looked up at the doctor.

"Terrible?"

"Come on, Doc. You find out that your parents died in an automobile accident, wouldn't you be upset?"

There was silence in the room. Dr. Marks just looked at me.

"I was just watching television when the doorbell rang. I opened the door and saw two policemen. I was frightened, and then they asked if they could enter the house. They walked in and asked if I was alone. They told me what had happened. There wasn't anything I could do."

"You felt …"?

"There was nothing I could do. I felt helpless. Maybe if they came straight home or let me pick up the prescription, they would still be alive today."

"Do you feel like you were somehow responsible for what happened to them?"

"Yes." I began to cry. "If I had insisted on picking up my own prescription, there might not have been that fucking accident."

"It sounds like you are quite angry at yourself."

"Yes, I am."

"John, they were returning home from a dinner party, and someone ran a stop sign?"

"Yes."

"If they had remained at the dinner party for several more minutes, the accident might not have happened. There are probably a hundred scenarios we can both think of that would have delayed their departure or accelerated it. Do you think you are taking responsibility for something that was out of your control?"

"I never thought of it that way, but I was just sitting at home and could have gone to the pharmacy."

"That isn't the issue."

I looked at Dr. Marks and said, "You mean I wasn't the one responsible for the accident? It was that driver."

Dr. Marks nodded.

I said, "Remember when we were speaking about 9/11? That wasn't my responsibility either. There was nothing I could have done."

"Yes, John, sometimes you are not expected to be in control."

I smiled, took a deep breath, and exhaled.

"That is about it for today, John. I will see you tomorrow."

"Thank you, Dr. Marks. I really appreciate what you are doing for me."

"You're welcome, John, but you are the one who is doing all the work!"

I walked out of the office and was feeling better. *I really need to explore the issue of control.* I left the building and immediately called Christina.

"John, is that you?"

"Yes. I just left the session, and there was a major breakthrough. I can't wait to tell you."

"That is wonderful, John! I am happy for you!"

"Dr. Marks knows what he is doing. Todd Lawson was right. I am glad I listened to him. What a relief. I wish you were here right now. I want to kiss you. I haven't felt this good in years—actually since my parents died."

"John, you sound like you are going to explode with joy."

"No, Christina, I am already there."

"I just received a call from Scott."

"What did you say?"

"He wanted to speak to you. I told him you were in the city and wouldn't be home until six thirty. He said you could call him when you arrived home. This time, I wrote down his telephone number."

"That is splendid. I can't wait to speak to him. I will see you within two hours, Christina. I love you."

I was in luck that afternoon. I did not have to wait long for the train. On my way home, I thought about my session and what Dr. Marks had said. *How could I have been so foolish? For all those years, I blamed myself. It took a major crisis and counseling for me to come to terms with what really happened. I felt bad about my parents and grieved their deaths, but I no longer have to blame myself.*

I was looking forward to speaking to Scott. I knew that would be the best medicine for me. I missed him. I was wondering how he was doing. I hoped he had some good news to share with me. I looked out the window and felt like things were changing in my life for the better.

When I arrived at the station, Christina was waiting for me.

I ran over and gave her a hug and kiss. I was bursting with excitement.

When we arrived home, Christina went into the kitchen and turned on the television. She said she would begin preparing dinner.

I kissed her and glanced at the news. "Christina, you know I do not want to watch the television. I find that shit upsetting. They keep on replaying the same thing over and over again. Look at that. They are interviewing people who lost a loved one. I just want to throw a brick through that set!"

Christina slowly walked over to the television and shut it off.

"It is too late for that. I am already upset. I had such a good day too. I am going to take a shower."

"How about dinner? It will be ruined," Christina said.

"I've lost my appetite." I left the kitchen.

Christina yelled, "You are supposed to call Scott."

"It will just have to wait."

I walked back into the kitchen and saw Christina sobbing at the table.

"What's wrong?"

Christina ignored me.

"Christina, I am speaking to you."

Christina looked at me and said, "Yes, you are. You are so wrapped up in yourself, and you don't seem to care about those around you. The other day, you were so concerned about hurting the baby physically, but don't you realize that emotion may play a role as well? Look at me." Christina's eyes were bloodshot and swollen. Tears were running down her face.

I walked over to her.

She backed away and said, "I prepared a beautiful dinner, and you chose to go on a tirade because of the television being on. I am sorry if I like a little company while I prepare dinner. You don't realize or appreciate all I do for you. I worked, went food shopping, and cooked. I am thankful for what I thought was progress, but I can't go through this anymore. It is too much for me to handle. I feel like going to my mother's until you cool down."

I slowly approached Christina and took a deep breath. *What the fuck did I do? She is a very special woman and the mother of my child. How can I treat her this way? I thought I was moving forward. What got into me? That is just a television, and it is reporting life as it is. I need to accept it and move on. I cannot let myself stall out emotionally. I must get it together—no matter what it takes.*

I looked into Christina's eyes and said, "I am so sorry. I don't know what got into me. I must get a better handle on these things. I do not want to lose you. Why don't I get washed up, and then we can have dinner together?"

Christina said, "John, I understand what you are going through—and I support you—but you can't victimize me anymore. I can't allow it. Do you understand?"

I began to realize that I had gone too far. "I don't want to hurt you. I really don't. It is all this emotion inside of me. At times, I can't control it. I don't know what to do."

"John, I do not want to hear any excuses. It is what it is. I am telling you I love you and want to be with you, but I can't get upset like this. It is not good for the baby or me. I am not threatening you, but you may need some time alone."

I took another step close to Christina and whispered, "I love you and want to be with you. I promise I will work on it. I will." I put my arms around her.

Her body stiffened.

"Please, Christina, give me another chance."

Pulling herself away, Christina replied, "John, this isn't about chances. This is about the quality of life we choose for ourselves. I want peace and tranquility. This drama is too much. This is it. I will not discuss this with you again. Next time, I am out of here until you get it together. Do you understand?"

"Yes, Christina. I will try. I promise you I will make us work again." I reached down and kissed her cheek. "I will be right back."

When I returned to the kitchen, dinner was on the table.

Christina was eating her salad. "Welcome back, John," she said.

I kissed her head and sat down. "This looks like a lovely dinner. Actually, it is my favorite. Thank you. The steak is good, and you made fries too. What more can I ask?"

"Probably for a warm dinner," she said.

"Christina, it is good. You made a great dinner, and I appreciate it. We have a lot to be thankful for, don't we?"

"We sure do."

CHAPTER SEVENTEEN
A CONVERSATION WITH SCOTT

At seven forty-five, I returned Scott's call. I had just finished helping Christina with the dinner dishes. I was nervous when I began to dial.

"Hello?"

"Scott, is that you?"

"Yes," Scott replied.

"It is good to hear your voice," I said.

"The same here. How have you been?"

Scott indicated that he was not doing well. He was having difficulty settling down.

"I know what you mean."

Scott said, "I am driving my wife crazy. I have been irritable and argumentative. The children are also getting on my nerves. Don't get me wrong—I love them, but I am angry."

I felt bad for my friend. Scott was attempting to work through his issues by himself. He was not as fortunate as I was. Scott did not have the opportunity to speak to a professional. "So, it has been hard for you?" I asked.

"Yes, but I am getting by—and you?"

"It has been up and down. I feel like a yo-yo."

"What do you mean?"

"Sometimes I am good, and sometimes I am terrible. Today, for example, I was doing great—and then I came home and had a big fight with Christina because she was watching the news. Listening to people who have experienced what we have or worse upsets me. I get all worked up."

"Yes, I know what you mean. I am the same way," Scott replied.

"You know something? I miss having you around. We seem to understand one another, and that is very comforting to me. I still think back to that day. Do you?"

"Yes, how we managed to get home was a miracle," Scott said.

"Those train cars were so crowded, and the sweat was pouring off us. Scott, you were a great person to have around. I really appreciated it."

"John, you are no slouch. I couldn't have done it without you."

"Scott, do you suffer from any flashbacks or nightmares?"

"I probably do. I did not go through what you did, but I still have nightmares about our experience. I feel like I am on a train, and I cannot get to where I am going. It is quite disturbing. What is going on with you?"

Christina walked into the bedroom, and when she noticed that I was on the telephone, she turned around and walked out.

"I have been having major flashbacks. It seems real to me. My whole body shakes. I cannot get out of my mind the people jumping out of the window and their bodies splashing on the sidewalks when they hit the ground."

"Oh, I did not realize you were so close," Scott said.

"Yes. I tried to go into the building, and they turned me away. I now realize there was nothing I could have done. It was too late."

"That is terrible, John. It must have been very upsetting for you. I am sorry."

"I am getting through it. I have been very fortunate. My boss has insisted that I speak to a counselor who deals with situations like mine. They call it crisis intervention. It has really been helpful to me. I have only spoken to him two times, but it has already made a big difference. Maybe you should consider speaking to somebody."

"Me?"

"Yeah, you. Why not?"

"No. I don't need to speak to anyone."

"I thought the same thing. I have always been my own person.

I questioned the value of counseling, but it is really working for me. I cannot imagine where I would be if I did not have a trained professional to speak to about my concerns."

"John, I know you are trying to be helpful, but I am not that type of guy."

"You know what my wife told me?"

"What?"

"'Why not try it? You have nothing to lose—and everything to gain. If you do not like it, just discontinue with the process.' Doesn't that make sense?"

"I guess it does, but how do you go about finding the right person?"

I told him I would ask my doctor for a referral. Maybe he would know of someone in New Rochelle.

Scott thanked me.

"No problem, Scott. Do you think it would be a good idea for our wives to arrange a date when we can all get together?"

"Yes. We should put them on the telephone. They are the ones who keep the social calendars."

"Okay, I will get Christina. By the way, I never did ask your wife's name."

"It is Lynda. I will go get her."

"Christina," I yelled.

"Yes?" she called out from the kitchen.

"Can you come in here for a moment please? Bring the calendar too. I have Scott's wife on the phone."

Christina entered the bedroom.

"Yes, this is John. You must be Lynda. I am looking forward to meeting you. Just a minute, my wife is right here." I handed the telephone to Christina.

"Hi, I am Christina. It seems that the guys want us all to get together. Yes, that will be nice. Why don't you come here for dinner? Next Tuesday at seven—or maybe seven thirty will be better because of the traffic? No problem, I like to cook. Do you have any dietary restrictions? You do not need to bring anything—just yourselves. You are busy with the children and all. Okay then, looking forward to meeting you next week. Are the men done speaking? I guess they are then. Good night."

Christina turned to me and said, "She sounds nice."

"Thanks, Christina. That meant a lot to me." I walked over and kissed her.

"No problem, John."

Christina still seemed a little aloof. I could understand why. I was about to speak to her when the telephone rang.

She picked up the telephone. "Hi, Shirley. Yes, I met Richard, and he said something about getting together." Christina looked at me, shrugged, and motioned with her hand. "You would like us to come over to your house tomorrow evening? If you can hold on for a moment, I will speak to John."

I looked at Christina and hesitantly nodded.

"That seems fine. We will see you about seven. See you then." She hung up the telephone and said, "John, you seem somewhat reluctant."

"I never know what time I will be home because of the sessions."

"I realized that, but for the past two evenings, you've been home by six."

I looked up at Christina and said, "I guess you are right. What time do we have to be over at your friend's house?"

Christina replied, "Seven."

"It should be fine. Let's not make it an issue please."

"Okay. How is Scott?"

"Thanks for asking. He's trying to hang in there, but it is difficult. I am going to ask Dr. Marks for a referral in the New Rochelle area for him."

"That sounds good."

"I am going to shower now."

"I'll watch some television until you come out of the bathroom. Can we watch a movie?"

I was in the bathroom for close to forty-five minutes. By the time I came out, it was close to ten. "Christina, why don't we discuss children names?"

"That sounds good to me. What do you have in mind?"

We discussed names until midnight, but we didn't settle on one. We were both tired and went to bed.

I fell into a deep sleep and began to dream.

I was in New York City. There was thick smoke coming from the subway car. I could not breathe. I was choking. I was the only person in the train car. The doors were shut, and I could not escape. I tried to pry the doors open, but I couldn't get them to budge. I tried the emergency window release, but I burned my hand. I took off my coat and grabbed the latch, but it was stuck. There were people outside the car, but they were just standing there. I tried to signal to them by banging on the window, but they did not react. I began to yell as the smoke became denser.

"John, get up, get up," Christina said as she shook me.

I screamed, "Get me out of here. I need help."

Christina turned on the lamp and pushed and prodded me several times.

I opened my eyes and stared into Christina's eyes. "Was I having another bad nightmare?"

"Yes, sweetheart. You were. This time, I had difficultly waking you up. It took several minutes."

"I am sorry I awakened you. It was probably my conversation with Scott. We were talking about what happened."

"John, you ought to try to get back to sleep. You have to go into the city in the morning."

"That is a good idea."

She gave me a kiss and rubbed my back.

I turned over and fell asleep.

CHAPTER EIGHTEEN

THE THIRD SESSION

I slept well for the rest of the evening, and Christina was still sleeping when I awakened. I decided to skip my shower, quietly dress, and leave for the station. I left a note for Christina:

> Christina,
>
> Sorry for disturbing you last evening. Thought you could use your rest this morning. Have a great day. Looking forward to this evening. I love you.
>
> John

I thought I would grab something to eat on my way to work. I really did not want to make noise in the kitchen and disturb Christina.

The train ride was uneventful. I stood until a seat became available. I stopped for a light breakfast at the deli, and then I walked over to the office. When I arrived, I began thinking about what I was going to discuss with Dr. Marks. What came to my mind was what had happened the previous night. I began to feel unsettled.

I was a few minutes early, and I picked up a magazine and started to leaf through it until I heard my name called.

The receptionist said, "You can go in now."

I walked into the office and sat down on my usual chair. A cup of tea was waiting for me on the table. Dr. Marks entered the office, and I stood up.

"John, you do not need to be so formal," Dr. Marks said jokingly as he sat down.

I nodded. "Good morning."

"And a good morning to you, John. You look like there is something on your mind?"

"There is, Dr. Marks."

"What is it?"

"I was feeling great after yesterday's session. I left the office and felt full of energy. I had not felt that way for many years."

"Many years?"

"Yes, since my parents died. I was exuberant. I called Christina and told her how I was feeling. She picked me up at the train station, and I was glad to see her. When we arrived home, Christina turned on the television, and when I saw the news, I blew up and yelled at her."

"John, how were you feeling?"

"I was pissed off. She was watching the news."

"What did you see?"

"They were interviewing a young woman about the World Trade Center."

"What upset you about that?"

"It brought back all those associations—especially the people jumping out of the building and splattering all over the sidewalk."

"That must have been very difficult for you."

"It was, and I was angry at Christina for watching it."

"At Christina. What do you mean?" Dr. Marks asked.

"She put the television on, didn't she?"

"Yes, but she did not have any responsibility for what they were broadcasting, did she?"

"It sounds like you are supporting what she did," I said.

"John, is the issue whose side I am taking—or what really happened in that situation?"

"I guess you are right."

"Right about what?" Dr. Marks asked.

"That this is more about my anger and not about Christina turning on the television."

"Perhaps it is more about being out of control."

"Yeah, I really did lose control."

"And?"

"I yelled at Christina. She had no idea how I would react. She really did not think about it before she turned on the television. She said she just wanted some company while she was preparing dinner."

"What would have been a better way of handling the situation?"

"Saying nothing."

"John, do you really think that would be helpful to you or Christina? You were very disturbed about what you saw."

"I did tell her that I did not like to watch the television, especially the news."

"You explained it to her?"

"No, I yelled at her."

"Something tells me she is not aware of what you were really experiencing. Did you share your flashbacks with her?"

"No, I didn't."

"John, you look guilty. Your facial expression and your eyes are communicating that to me. That is not the point of this conversation. What do you think is the essence?"

"I think the situation could have been handled differently."

Dr. Marks paused for a moment and there was silence in the room.

John looked up at him and said, "I could have verbalized what I was experiencing instead of yelling at her."

Dr. Marks nodded his head yes. "What is more important is that you are still experiencing flashbacks. We've discussed them some already, and you do have greater insight, but you are still having them, and they are very disturbing."

"I also had a horrible nightmare last night."

"Can you tell me about it?"

"I was trapped in a subway car, and it was filling with smoke. I could not breathe. I was choking. I could not get out. There were people outside the train car, but they were not reacting to my calls for help."

"How did it make you feel?"

"I felt helpless and scared. No one was willing to help me. I also felt a loss of control."

"A loss of control?"

"Yes. I should have been able to get out of that car and free myself. I was suffocating."

"Did you recognize anyone?"

"I hadn't given that much thought. Wait a minute." I closed my eyes. "There was a blonde woman, a man with dark hair, and several other people."

"Did they remind you of anyone?"

"I guess in sort of an abstract way. The blonde woman could have been Christina and the dark-haired guy could have been you."

Dr. Marks looked at me and waited for my response.

I looked toward the window and a strange feeling traveled down my body. I stared into space and looked back at the doctor. "I wanted to be able to get out of the situation, but there was no help—not from the woman or the man."

"It sounds like you were very frustrated and frightened," Dr. Marks remarked.

"And no one seemed to understand or want to help me," I said.

"It sometimes feels that way, doesn't it, John?" Dr. Marks looked at me.

"Yes, it does. I guess I am impatient and want quicker results. I want you and Christina to do something for me. I want this whole situation behind me—so I can get on with my life."

"Yes, I understand that. This whole process has not been easy for you. You want others to help you—and you feel disappointed in them?"

"Exactly."

"So, you feel like we could be doing more for you?"

"It is not your fault, Doc. It is me," I said.

"John, it is all right if you feel that way, but I am partially responsible. That is how you feel, and no one can take that away from you. You should not feel guilty about it. We are going to deal with it. These are very complicated situations that we are trying to work on together, and it will take time. You are doing well, considering the intensity and magnitude of the trauma you experienced."

"Doc, what is wrong with me? Am I going crazy? I seem to hurt those I love. If you could have seen Christina's face last night after I yelled at her."

"No, John, you are not crazy, you are suffering from a condition that is called PTSD or post-traumatic stress disorder."

"Is it curable?"

Dr. Marks looked me and said, "Considering your intellect and emotional capacity, your condition will improve with time. You will need to be more patient and let those who love and care about you give you support so you will have the strength to persevere. I know you can do it. Give yourself a chance. You really have come a long way in a short period of time. It takes a team of players to win a game."

I looked up at him. "I know I can do it—and I want to succeed."

"That is great. In fact, I have good news for you. Starting tomorrow, you will spend two hours a day in the office. How do you feel about that?"

I smiled and said, "I was wondering when that was going to happen." I began to wonder if I would be able to assume that degree of responsibility. I turned to Dr. Marks. "Do you think I am ready?"

"What do you think, John?"

"I have been bored and would like to return to the workplace."

"What is holding you back?"

"I guess I am."

"John, it is two hours."

"I really would like to try. What time are they expecting me?"

Dr. Marks smiled. "You will report to work in the late morning and come to my office in the afternoon to discuss how things worked out. How does that sound to you?"

"That sounds good to me."

"Doc, there is something I forgot to tell you."

"Yes, John."

"Last evening, I spoke to Scott. He needs to speak to someone like you. The problem is that he lives in New Rochelle. Would it be possible for you to recommend someone?"

"John, it may take a few days, but I will get back to you. Do you want to discuss your conversation with Scott? If I am not mistaken, he was with you on 9/11."

"Yes, that is correct. It was great speaking to him. It was as if we were back on the subway together. Well, maybe not that horrible, crowded, suffocating, and unbearable subway."

"Suffocating?"

I smiled. "We commiserated for an hour. He is having difficulties too, and that is why I recommended that he speak to someone. At first, he was against it, but I told him how helpful it was for me. I suggested that he just try counseling. I pointed out that if he was not comfortable with the process, he could discuss it with the counselor."

"John, you seem very concerned about your friend."

"Yes, it was nice speaking to him, but he did not seem right to me. He lacked the confidence he had when we were together."

"Not everyone experiences immediate results from treatment. Many factors determine one's progress."

"Yes, I realize that, but he really needs to speak to someone. His issues have begun to interfere with his personal life. We never spoke about his job. Can you imagine that? We spent an hour on the telephone, and we never discussed it."

"John, it is sometimes amazing how conversations flow."

"I know what you mean. Look at us. I sometimes think we are going to discuss one thing, and we wind up talking about something else. I am so glad that Todd Lawson has asked me back to work. It means so much to me. I will not let him down."

"John that will be it for today. Good luck tomorrow. Have a good evening. Ah, before you go, I would like you to think about something."

I looked at Dr. Marks.

"I would like Christina to join us at a time that is convenient for both of you. Are you okay with that?"

"I do not see a problem. I will speak to her about it tonight."

Dr. Marks and I stood up.

I said goodbye and exited the office. I felt excited about getting back to work. I wondered what Mr. Lawson would have me doing. I stood in the lobby for a moment and watched the people leaving the building.

I walked to Grand Central Station. I could not wait to get home. When I called Christina, she reminded me of the date we had with Richard and Shirley. On my way home from the station, I purchased a dozen roses and had them wrapped. I attached a note.

Thank you for being you.

Love you forever.

John

I walked into the house and called out, "Christina, are you here?" The laundry was folded and piled up on the dryer.

"Just a minute—I am in the bedroom. I'm getting ready for tonight."

I walked into the bedroom with the flowers behind my back. "How are you doing?"

Christina said, "I am fine."

"Did you have a nice day at work?" I asked.

"Yes, things went well. I was assigned a new project. It looks like it is going to be a challenge. I was hoping they would choose my team. It is a big account, and there is a possibility of a promotion if I do a good job."

"I have something for you that will make your day even better." I presented her with the bouquet of roses.

She walked over to me and said, "They are beautiful." She gave me a kiss and fell into my arms. "I will put these beautiful flowers in water as soon as I put on my other shoe."

I smiled. "Christina, Dr. Marks asked if you would join us for a session."

Christina thought for a minute and then said, "John, I would love to, but I am starting the new project next week. I will not be able to take any time off from work. I really do want to meet him. I know this is short notice, but how about tomorrow?"

"Christina, I was asked to return to work tomorrow for a few hours. I will be meeting with Dr. Marks after that."

"What time will that be?"

"About eleven."

"That is perfect. I will take a long lunch and meet you there."

"I did not inform him that you will be joining us."

"Don't worry, John. I am sure it will be all right. It is just a formality to let him know. I am sure he is flexible."

"I guess you are right."

"Great. I will be there at eleven. Just remind me of the address."

"I will write it down for you."

"That will be wonderful. John, I thought we might be in a hurry tonight. I picked up a pizza on the way home, and I prepared a salad. It is in the refrigerator."

"That is fine. Are Richard and Shirley having anyone else over this evening?"

"I do not think so, but I really do not know."

"I would just appreciate one thing."

Christina cut off the ends of the roses and placed them in a vase. "What might that be?"

"Tomorrow is a workday, and I would like to get home relatively early."

Christina replied, "No problem, John. I really never liked going out during the week, but it has been a while since we accepted an invitation from them. I did not want to seem rude to them, and I think I mentioned to Shirley that it was a work night."

I smiled at Christina and gave her kiss. "I should have realized that you would have thought about that." I sat down, opened the box of pizza, and placed a slice on each of our plates.

"Thanks, John," she said.

"No problem. Would you like some salad? It looks delicious. I especially like all those chopped vegetables. It must have taken you forever." I used the serving spoons to serve the salad.

"No thanks, John. I had a large salad for lunch today."

I placed her salad back in the bowl. "Christina, I was so excited today when Dr. Marks asked me to return to work. I can't wait to get involved. I have been wondering what Todd is going to have me do."

"It sounds like they feel you are ready, and that is a good thing."

"Yes. I have been so bored, and my sessions are going well. Last night was just an unfortunate situation. We spoke today, and I have a handle on it."

"I can see that, John, and I am thankful and pleased."

"Thanks, Christina." I reached over and gave her a kiss. "I wish we were staying home tonight."

"John," Christina said.

"No, Christina. I am looking forward to going, but I would like to be with you."

"John, it is only six, and we don't have to be there for an hour."

I loosened my tie, slipped it over my head, and began to unbutton my shirt. "Let's not waste any time then."

An hour later, we emerged from the bedroom and were ready to go to our friends' house.

The evening went well. Christina and I brought a bottle of wine, but no one wanted to indulge. Richard and I spoke about sports and our jobs. The women discussed their newest exercise programs. Christina also shared her news about her new account at work.

Shirley served pastries and coffee, and we all enjoyed a few laughs. The time went by quickly. We left around ten thirty, and we were home by ten forty-five. It had just begun to rain when we entered the garage.

Christina finished in the kitchen while I got ready for bed. I straightened the sheets and blankets and climbed into bed.

When Christina joined me, she gave me a kiss and said, "Thank you for the roses and a nice evening."

CHAPTER NINETEEN
WORK

I arrived at the office early the next morning. I was excited about beginning work. It had been a while, and I was looking forward to interacting with other people. I walked over to Todd Lawson's office and addressed the secretary who was sipping on a cup of coffee and eating a doughnut. "Is he in?"

She wiped her mouth with a napkin and said, "Yes. He is expecting you. Go right in."

I opened the door and walked into Todd's office. "Good morning."

"John, you seem energetic this morning and ready to start your day. That is great." Todd had several things he wanted me to do. He asked me to review twenty résumés. There had been sixty, but he had already eliminated forty. The remaining ones were good candidates for the new program that he wanted me to run. It was going to be a training program for account executives who would be reviewing and servicing accounts. After choosing the top fifteen candidates, we could meet and discuss them.

I told him that I would contact him after I completed the process.

Todd asked me to complete the process as soon as possible.

I informed him that I would speak to him after I finished.

He told me not to rush and to be as thorough as I could be. If I finished that day, it would be fine. If not, there was always tomorrow. Todd requested that I work in the cubicle next to his office. He told me to let him know if I had any questions.

Todd handed me the résumés, and I sat down in the cubicle.

The workspace was small and somewhat confining, but it would be sufficient for my needs. I began to review the résumés. I read the documents and wrote my comments directly on them. The candidates were very impressive. The time flew by.

Todd walked into the cubicle. "How are you doing?"

"Just fine. We have some really good candidates here. I just have a few more to go. I should complete the process in about twenty minutes."

Todd looked at his watch. "That will be fine then. You have about half an hour. Why don't you finish up—and we can meet tomorrow in my office at nine?"

"That sounds good," I said.

"John, be sure to be cognizant of the time. Your appointment is at eleven."

"Of course. No problem." I said.

Todd left, and I continued reading the résumés. When I was finished, I sorted them from the best to the worst candidates. I then placed the résumés in a drawer and left the office. I was proud of my accomplishment and was looking forward to my meeting with Todd.

CHAPTER TWENTY

THE JOINT SESSION

I arrived at eleven o'clock for my appointment. When I walked into the office, Christina was in the reception area. I greeted her with a kiss and told her that she looked beautiful.

"When did you get here?" I asked.

"A few minutes ago," she said.

I sat down next to her. "Did you have any trouble finding the office?"

"No."

The receptionist looked at me and said, "You can go in. Dr. Marks is ready for you."

I opened the door, and we walked into Dr. Marks's office. Dr. Marks was standing by his desk. He smiled and said, "You must be Christina. Splendid that you are able to join us today."

Christina looked at me and smiled.

"Why don't you sit down? Would you like anything to drink, Christina?"

"No, thank you. I am fine." Christina looked at Dr. Marks and said, "I am sorry about the short notice, but I am starting a new project next week and will not be able to take any time off."

"No problem, Christina. You do not need to apologize. I am just thankful that you are here. Why don't you begin by telling me how you two met?"

Christina said, "It was a blind date. Our mutual friends thought it would be a good if we met. John called me one evening, and we decided to have coffee."

"How did that first encounter go?"

Christina smiled and said, "It went great. John was—and is—a really nice guy."

"What do you mean?"

"Look at him." Her eyes began to sparkle. "He is tall, well built, and handsome. I was very attracted to him. Unlike other men I had dated, he was smart, sensitive, and caring."

"And how did you feel about Christina, John?"

"I was very attracted to her, especially her wit."

"Her wit?"

"Yes. She can be funny and sarcastic. Christina is a real challenge to me. She is also beautiful. Just look at those blue eyes."

He turned to her and smiled. "Would you say, after a year of marriage, that you are both compatible with one another?"

I looked at Dr. Marks and said. "She is everything I could ever want. She is beautiful, smart, loving, caring, direct, and a very hard worker. We are compatible mentally, socially, and sexually. We share common interests such as sports, theater, and exercising."

Christina looked down and clutched her hands. Tears began to form in her eyes.

"Christina, you seem taken aback by what John just said," Dr. Marks said.

"Yes, I am. Everything seemed perfect, especially after he worked through his concerns centering around the death of his parents several years ago. Then there was that horrific day. John just has not been right."

As I was listening to what Christina was saying, I felt concerned. I had never thought of our relationship in those terms.

"Christina, what do you mean?"

"Everything was wonderful. John was sensitive and caring. He was always there for me. He helped around the house and did little things I really liked. Before he left for work on 9/11, he left a note on the table. It was our anniversary, and he had made reservations at our favorite restaurant. It was about us—not just him."

"Him?"

"Yes. After 9/11, it is all about him. He has been miserable, angry, and depressed. Nothing seems to satisfy him. Nothing. I try so hard, but nothing is working. Whatever I do, it is never good enough."

I started to cry.

Christina said, "He is irritable and short. He experiences temper outbursts. Even the thought of our baby does not seem to make him happy. Don't get me wrong—he isn't this way all of the time. Sometimes he is the old John, but at other times, he is this uncontrollable, excuse me, bastard." Christina began to cry. "He doesn't realize what I was going through; 9/11 was no picnic for me. I was worrying all day. I did not know if he was alive or dead. If it weren't for my mother and a friend, I would have been in worse shape than he was."

"Christina, this time has been very difficult for you as well," Dr. Marks said.

"Yes, it has. He has made progress since he began speaking with you. He likes you, and I believe the process has been a good one. At times, he is happy and appears content, but at other times, he is upset."

"I am glad to hear there has been progress. John, what do you think?"

I wiped my eyes and blew my nose. "Christina, I didn't realize how bad it was until the other night when I blew up. Even then, I was unaware of the extent of the problem. I just could not help myself."

Christina reached for my hand.

I thought, *She is everything a man could ever dream of having. Christina is a loving and caring wife. She doesn't deserve to be abused by anyone—let alone the man who loves her. She is one in a million.* I began to cry again and reached out for her hand.

Christina said, "It is all right, John. I know you could not help it. That is why I thought you needed to speak to someone about your concerns. What you went through was awful and would be too much for anyone to endure. You are getting through it. Dr. Marks is here to help you—and us. We will get back to where we once were. It may take time, but we will get there."

Dr. Marks said, "Yes, you will. John, it is essential that you do not feel guilty. That will immobilize you. Accept what has happened and move on. I know that is easier said than done, but you have what it takes. You are a fighter and a born leader who succeeds and wins trophies."

I nodded.

"This is another step forward. Be honest and lay everything out on the table. The man who walked into my office several days ago is a different one than the one who is sitting here now. Look at all you have accomplished. You are even working."

I nodded.

"What are you thinking, John?"

I stared out the window. I felt warm, and I was sweating. "It is so much to digest. I am really trying, but sometimes, it is still hard, especially when I see or hear things that remind me of that day. My whole body quivers. It is better, but it is still an issue. I do not want to be a burden to Christina. It is not her responsibility to take care of me. I don't want a mother. I want a wife. I must succeed. I have a new baby on the way. I can't fail. I will not let myself. There are a lot of things I want to do with my life. I know I have a great deal to give. I was spared, and there must be a reason for that."

"Spared, John?"

"I could have been in a meeting in my office if that subway did not arrive late to the station. The Lord evidently had other plans for me. I will not let him down."

Christina said, "John, it is important that you don't let yourself down. Use whatever guidance you think he has given you and forge ahead."

"Yes. You are right—it is up to me."

Dr. Marks said, "And?"

"Yes, of course, Christina. I would not be able to survive without her. We are a team and soon will be a trio."

"When are you expecting your child?" Dr. Marks asked.

Christina said, "In late spring. We are uncertain of the exact date. We have only had one appointment."

"Christina, is there anything else you would like to say to John?" Dr. Marks asked.

"Yes. John, you told me that Scott understood you. It made me feel like I would never be able to grasp the things you experienced the way he did. How do you think that made me feel?"

"Christina, I did not mean it that way."

"That was what you said."

"I meant that he and I shared the experience together. In addition, he is a guy. We just relate differently."

"Do you hear yourself, John? My not being a guy rules out the possibility that I would be able to understand you. Perhaps it is not me who has that difficulty—it is your inability to share what happened. If you do not speak to me, how do you expect me to gain any insight into how you are feeling? John, you met Scott *after* you experienced the situation. You were at the bridge."

"Oh, I never looked at it that way. I feel confused."

Christina said, "No, John. You do not want to talk about it. You are withdrawing."

Dr. Marks said, "Does that make sense to you, John?"

I gazed out the window. I felt flushed. I turned to Christina and said, "I do believe that Scott and I connected, and that was special."

Christina said, "There is no doubt that you and he were able to relate well to one another, but that doesn't diminish our capacity to speak to one another. It is no different than how you might have related to different guys on your team."

"Yes. I see what you are saying. Perhaps it is me and how I choose to communicate with the people around me."

"Exactly John," Dr. Marks said. "It is a learning process."

"Hmm," I said.

Dr. Marks said, "John, Christina brought up another important point. Do you remember what she said?"

I thought for a while. There had been so much said, and I felt overloaded. "I encountered Scott *after* the situation and crisis."

Dr. Marks nodded.

I said, "That is correct, but in my mind, the event was still happening. Yes, it was replaying in my head like a newsreel over and over again. Do you understand it was still happening? Just like when I had the flashbacks. It put me back to ground zero. It is not something I wanted to do—it just happened."

Dr. Marks answered, "Yes, John. I understand."

"So do I," Christina added.

"Christina, is there anything else you would like to add today?" Dr. Marks asked.

"No, Dr. Marks. This has been a very enlightening session for me. Thank you for including me. I appreciate it." Christina kissed John. "I have to return to work. I will see you at home."

"Thank you, Christina, I will see you later."

Christina walked toward the door, opened it and winked at me.

After she closed the door, Dr. Marks said, "What did you think of our session? Was it what you expected?"

"I knew Christina had a number of things she wanted to discuss, but I was not aware of how upset she was. It was helpful to better understand her point of view. As time goes by, I will learn to deal with the issues better, and that will improve our relationship. I need to be more open, especially about what happened to me. I am just frightened that it will result in flashbacks and nightmares. That is what happened the other night when I spoke to Scott."

"John, that is a risk, but there is something we might be able to do about it."

"What do you have in mind?"

Dr. Marks said, "There is this process called *desensitization*, which might be helpful."

I leaned forward and said, "Tell me more."

Dr. Marks said, "Desensitization is a therapeutic process in which an individual is placed in a relaxed state, and then the traumatic event is presented through visual imagery in a gradient from mild to severe. When the individual experiences anxiety, he or she is placed back into the relaxed state of mind. Eventually, the discomfort from the traumatic events is reduced in intensity. Do you understand, John?"

"Yes, I do. When can we start?" I wanted to begin immediately.

"Are you up for it now?"

I said, "I think so. I am very eager to start."

"John, tell me one of the places where you feel the most relaxed?"

"At the seashore."

"The chair you are sitting on is a recliner. Lean back all the way. You are going to do a relaxation exercise. When I instruct you, I want you to close your eyes. I am going to ask you to tighten certain muscles and then relax them very slowly. Let me demonstrate." Dr. Marks tightened one of his hands into a fist. He then very slowly opened it and rested it on his chair. "Be sure to open your hand very slowly. Do you understand?"

I nodded. "Yes. I think I got it."

"I am going to start with the muscles of your head and face and work down to your feet and legs. I am going to have you indicate how relaxed you are with your index finger. Let me show you. If you are totally relaxed, you will rest your finger on the chair like this." Dr. Marks demonstrated. "If you are very anxious, I want you to elevate your finger like this. As long as you are feeling tense or upset, keep your finger elevated. When you begin to feel relaxed, lower it. Do you have any questions?"

"No."

"Okay then," Dr. Marks said. "Close your eyes and take a deep breath."

I closed my eyes and took a very deep breath.

"That's good. Now let it out very slowly."

I quickly exhaled.

"No, John. I want you to exhale very slowly. Let's try it again. Be sure to keep your eyes closed. Take a deep breath.

"That is good. Now exhale. Great. I want you to do it one more time. Take a deep breath, hold it, hold it, and now very slowly exhale. You can feel a relaxing sensation traveling down your whole body from your head and face to your neck and shoulders, arms and hands, stomach, and now your feet and legs. You are feeling more and more relaxed. Now tense the muscles of your head and face ... tighter, tighter, hold, hold. And now relax. You can feel a relaxing sensation traveling down your whole body from your head and face ... to your neck and shoulders to your arms and hands to your stomach ... and now your feet and legs. Your whole body is feeling more and more relaxed and at peace and at rest."

As Dr. Marks continued down my body, I was feeling more and more relaxed. My body was limp.

"And now your feet and legs. Tense them up ... hold ... hold ... and now relax. You can feel a relaxing sensation traveling down your whole body from your head to your neck and shoulders, to your arms and hands, your stomach, and now your feet and legs. Your whole body is at a state of total relaxation. Now, I would like you to picture yourself at the beach. It is a bright, sunny day, and you are looking out on to the cool, blue, crystal water. There is a slight breeze blowing against your face and through your hair. You can hear the water gently beating against the white sand. Your whole body is feeling more and more relaxed and at peace and rest."

Dr. Marks repeated the exercise one more time and then asked me to show him how relaxed I was. My index finger remained on the arm of the chair.

Dr. Marks said, "When you open your eyes, your whole body will be in a state of relaxation—and this feeling is going to stay and remain with you. Open your eyes."

I slowly opened my eyes and looked at Dr. Marks. It took a few seconds to adjust to the light. My eyes were heavy, and I felt like I wanted to go to sleep. "Boy, that felt good. I almost fell asleep several times."

Dr. Marks smiled. "You reacted well to the exercise. In fact, while I was speaking, I made you a tape. Here you are." He handed me a cassette tape. "Now you can practice at home, or if you are feeling a little unsettled, you can play it. Just go into a room where it is quiet, get into a comfortable position, close your eyes, and play the tape. This is the first phase of the exercise."

"Oh, there is more?"

"Yes, we have to assist you in dealing with the trauma and your subsequent anxiety and fears."

"Oh, I see. That ought to be very enlightening for me."

"I see you want to move on. Remember to be patient. It takes time, and you are doing very well. This has been a long session, and we have accomplished many things. Your reaction to the relaxation exercise was very positive. Thank you again for asking Christina to join us. I can see why you think she is a special woman. Please feel free to have her join us in the future. Have a good night. I will see you tomorrow after work. We are going to increase your time at work to three hours."

I looked at him and said, "Thank you so much for everything. I can't express my appreciation and gratitude enough."

Dr. Marks nodded. "By the way, John, here is the name of the doctor for your friend in New Rochelle."

"Thank you, Dr. Marks. I will certainly give it to him."

As I walked to the elevator, I felt more relaxed than I had in a long time. I smiled and walked to Grand Central Station.

CHAPTER TWENTY-ONE

DINNER FOR TWO

At seven o'clock, I arrived home. Christina knew I would be late. I had called from the station. In fact, Christina was still at work when I called.

When I entered through the garage into the kitchen, Christina was standing at the sink and said, "John, I don't know about you, but I am exhausted."

"Why don't we go out for dinner tonight?" I said.

"That sounds wonderful. No preparation—and no dishes."

"Where would you like to go? What do you feel like eating, Christina?"

"How about Chinese food?"

"I was just going to suggest that! Should we order in or go to the restaurant?"

"Why don't we order in? That will give me a chance to rest and put up my legs."

"No problem. What do you want to order?"

"Why don't you surprise me?"

I walked into the kitchen and called the Sun Mei Restaurant. "I would like to order. I would like a quart of wonton soup, roast pork with vegetables, and one shrimp with lobster sauce. That is it. Twenty minutes? I will be there." I walked into the family room.

Christina was sitting on the recliner with her feet up. I approached her and began massaging her feet.

"That is so heavenly. Thank you."

I was becoming excited, but I focused on what I was doing.

Christina closed her eyes and fell asleep.

I walked back into the kitchen, set the table with paper plates and plastic forks and spoons, and drove to the restaurant.

There was a small line of people waiting for their orders. They were apparently backed up in the kitchen. I began speaking to the woman in front of me. She was new to Connecticut and was wondering if I had ordered food from Sun Mei in the past. I told her I had—and that it was pretty good.

Several minutes later, my order was ready. I paid and left.

When I arrived home, I placed the bags on the table and walked into the family room.

Christina was still asleep. I gave her kiss. She opened her eyes, yawned, and stretched out her arms. "You better go pick up the food. It will be waiting."

"It is already here. It is on the kitchen table," I replied.

"Oh, great. I am starving—or should I say *we* are hungry?" Christina rubbed her stomach.

I smiled, and we walked into the kitchen.

"And you set the table? How considerate is that?" Christina smiled and kissed me on the cheek.

"What did you think of Dr. Marks?"

"He is a nice guy."

"Did you like him?"

"What do you mean? I really don't know him. He seems likeable. He appears to like you. I found him easy to speak to." Christina opened the container of soup and served us.

"Yeah, and I really like him. He has been very helpful to me. This soup is really good." I opened a bag of egg noodles, added them to the soup, and handed the bag to Christina.

"I can see that." Christina sprinkled some of the noodles into her bowl and continued eating.

"Dr. Marks taught me a relaxation exercise today."

"That is wonderful. Did it work?"

"Yes, I almost fell asleep in his office."

"I guess you were relaxed then."

"I have a tape that I can use at home. I am going to try it after dinner. I am looking forward to it. He told me it was phase one. He felt it could help me with my flashbacks and nightmares."

"That would be fantastic, John. He seemed to know what he was doing."

"There is more. Tomorrow, I will be starting to work for three hours a day. How was your day?"

Christina wiped her mouth with a napkin. Her blonde hair was pulled back, and her blue eyes sparkled. "This morning, I felt rushed. I did not want to be late for the appointment. I was concerned about how you would react to what I was saying to the doctor. I did not want to upset you."

"Christina, I appreciated what you said. I had not realized how much I had upset you. I learned a lot, and I will be more mindful of speaking to you more often about my feelings. You know that men are not really programmed that way. I learned to keep it all in—just like my father. I am supposed to be the strong man and not show any signs of weakness."

"That did not seem to be the case with Scott," She stated.

I thought for a moment. "You are right. I don't know why that happened. Perhaps it was the situation we were in at the time."

"That is irrational, John. You just contradicted yourself."

I was perplexed and thought for a moment and then said, "I will change. I am working on it, and for the betterment of our relationship, I have to learn how to tell you things so you can understand me. Right?"

"Yes, John. You are right. You have already begun the process, and you are doing well."

"Thank you, Christina. Would you like some tea? I can put up some water."

"Thanks, John, but I do not think it is a good idea for me to have the caffeine, especially at this time at night. Water would be nice."

"One water coming right up."

"You're chipper, John, for someone who is tired."

I was feeling energized. I felt like Christina and I had reached a breakthrough in our relationship. I looked at her and said, "You are so beautiful and wonderful. I enjoy speaking to you." I walked over to Christina and hugged her tightly.

Christina pulled back. "John, you are holding me too tight. I do not know what I am going to do with you. You are silly."

"No, I am happy to be with you—and I am looking forward to the birth of the baby."

Christina looked at me and smiled.

"Christina, go sit back down in the family room. I will clean up."

"Thank you, John. I appreciate it."

Christina walked into the family room, and I began to whistle as I cleaned up from dinner. I found the cassette player, placed it on the counter, and walked into the bedroom. I called to Christina and told her what I was doing.

She said, "Take your time."

I took off my tie, opened my shirt, repositioned the pillows, put on the headset, and turned on the tape. I soon fell fast asleep.

Christina walked into the bedroom, nudged me, and gave me a kiss, and I woke up. The headset fell off my head. "I told you I almost fell asleep. I guess I did this time."

"John, I think it would be a good idea for us to get undressed and get into bed. It has been a long day. We accomplished a great deal today. We have a lot to be thankful for at this time in our life."

I kissed Christina and hugged her gently.

We continued to kiss as we fell back into bed.

Christina turned off the lamp, and we held each other. We made love and fell asleep in each other's arms.

CHAPTER TWENTY-TWO

THE DREAM

I woke up at four o'clock in the morning and thought about my childhood. It was one of the best times of my life. I was an only child, and my parents loved me. They must have been financially comfortable, and I was wanting for nothing. My father was a sports enthusiast, and I was a well-coordinated kid. At an early age, I became interested in athletics. I fell asleep again and started to dream.

I was at home with my parents on a Saturday morning. I was in my bedroom.

My mother said, "John, it is time for breakfast."

I was playing with my toy soldiers and did not hear my mother's call. I continued playing. "Captain, is it time to attack? Yes, soldiers, on the count of three. One, two, three, charge!"

"John? It sounds like you are still playing. Your food is going to get cold. Please hurry down."

I smelled the aromas coming from the kitchen. "Pancakes? My favorite," I yelled. I was hungry. I ran down the stairs and gave my mother a big kiss on her cheek.

She looked into my eyes, reached down, and kissed me. "You are a mother's best little boy."

I looked at the table. "Those pancakes look good—and warm maple syrup?" I gulped them down.

"Sweetheart, there are plenty. Take your time."

I gazed at my mother, smiled, and took a sip of chocolate milk. "Gee, Mom, this is good. Thanks."

My dad entered the room. He was a tall, muscular man with blue eyes and grayish-brown curly hair. I said, "Hi, Pops."

"Good morning, John. Are you ready for soccer this morning?"

"Oh, I forgot."

"No problem. It is not until after lunch. We have plenty of time."

"Would you like some eggs?"

"Yes, Mom."

She cracked two eggs in a bowl, beat them with a fork, and placed some butter in the hot pan and it sizzled.

"I like the smell of the butter, Mom. Can I please have some with my toast?"

She dropped two pieces of rye bread into the toaster and scrambled the eggs.

I looked on with enthusiastic anticipation. I loved the taste of fresh eggs and buttered toast.

After breakfast, I returned to my room to play.

My father entered my room and said, "Would you like to practice soccer with me?"

"Sure, Pops," I said. "I will get dressed and be down right away."

My dad was very patient and supportive. He was an athlete and knew what training and coaching were all about.

I enjoyed playing with him. I picked up skills quickly and rarely complained about anything. My body was strong, and I was quite agile.

"John, I will stand in front of the goal, and you try to kick the ball into the net."

I awakened when Christina rolled over and hit me in the head. I turned over and closed my eyes and continued dreaming.

"John, are you going to the senior prom?" Charles was one of my good friends. He was short and stout. He was not very good at athletics, but he had a good sense of humor. We often argued, but we enjoyed each other's company.

"Yes, Charles. I am going with Diane."

"Oh, yeah? Going with the head cheerleader? Good choice. You will have a good chance of being crowned king and queen of the prom. Diane is really pretty. I can see why you asked her out. I didn't realize you were dating her so seriously."

"We weren't until several weeks ago. I think she wanted to go to the prom with me and was being extra nice to me—if you know what I mean."

"Can you explain more?" Charles asked.

"You will need to figure that out without my help," I said.

"Did you get a little?"

"Enough, Charles. By the way, who are you asking to the prom?"

"Mildred—and she gives great head."

"You and everyone else at school," I said jokingly. "I wonder what disease your cock is going to contract in the process."

"John, you always think the worst. You probably make the girls wear rubber gloves."

"You are a barrel of laughs, Charles. Just think of all those dicks she has had in her mouth before she placed her moist lips on you."

"John, perhaps next weekend you will have some fun and get to third base. Be sure to bring your rubbers."

"I guess if I forget, I can always borrow some from you—unless you go bareback."

"Not on your life. I am too young to have children."

"John, it is time to get up," Christina said. "You slept through the alarm."

I just wanted to go back to sleep. The dreams I was having made me feel so relaxed. Those were such carefree days with no responsibilities and lots of fun. I turned to Christina and said, "I hope I did not disturb you."

"That is all right. I had a restless sleep anyway. I couldn't find a comfortable position."

I sat up and got out of bed.

Christina smiled. "It looks like somebody is up to welcome the day."

I looked down. I was erect and peering out of my pajama bottoms. "Oh, Christina, it is just a morning thing. I wish I could be late for work, but that is not going to happen. You will need to wait until tonight."

"I am counting the minutes," Christina replied with a grin.

I arrived on time for work, took out the résumés, and reviewed them one more time. When I completed the process, I walked over to Todd Lawson's office.

Todd said, "Come in, John."

I handed him the résumés. "It has all been completed. I placed them in priority of excellence. The top one is the most impressive."

"John, thank you. I will take a look at them and get back to you today or tomorrow. I would like to speak to you first. Please sit down."

I approached the chair in front of the wooden desk and sat down.

Todd walked in front of the desk and sat down next to me. "John, how are you doing?"

"Great. I enjoyed reviewing the résumés, and I am looking forward to forming my team."

"No, John. I mean with the counseling?"

I was puzzled by the question since my sessions with Dr. Marks were supposed to be confidential.

"John, I am asking not as your employer but as a concerned friend."

I was slightly apprehensive, but I decided it would be best to continue the conversation. "It has been very interesting. Nothing like what I expected."

"What do you mean?"

"I thought Dr. Marks would focus on my childhood and parents. We briefly discussed it, but we have been mainly focused on the events of 9/11 and my reaction to them. Last session, my wife, Christina joined us. It went really well. I learned a lot of things about myself and the relationship."

"John, I am not asking you about the content of your sessions. I am concerned about how you are doing."

"It has been a struggle for me at times, but I am managing."

"What do you mean?" Todd said.

"Some days are better than others, but overall, I am making progress and feeling better. When I am here at work, I feel my best."

"You mean your job is a good divergence?"

"I think it might be that way for anyone, especially if he or she enjoys what he or she is doing. You have been very kind to me. I will always appreciate that. I am indebted to you."

"It is nice that you feel that way, but you deserve everything that is coming your way. You are a valued commodity around here, and I appreciate all you have done. Your reviews have been exceptional, and your coworkers respect you."

I said, "Yes, they did—and I miss them. But new workers will be taking their places soon. I hope I will form similar relationships with them."

Todd nodded. "John, thank you for sharing this with me. I appreciate your openness. Why don't we discuss the résumés now?"

Todd walked over to his desk and began to thumb through the papers. "John, thanks for writing these comments in the margins. It is really helpful to me. This fellow has exceptional skills. This woman has five years of experience. So many of these people will make great employees. I am going to ask my secretary to schedule appointments for the candidates in these piles. How much time will you need with each candidate?"

"I think forty-five minutes would be plenty. That includes meeting and greeting."

Todd smiled. "You certainly know how to put things in context,

John. Here is a job description. Why don't you glance at it while I give the résumés to my secretary?"

I looked over the three-page description.

Todd walked back into the office. "Do you have any questions?"

"No, Todd. It seems clear to me. After I meet with all the candidates. I will discuss my impressions with you."

"No, problem. We will set up a time for that. For the next few days, I would like you to work six hours a day so we can complete the process as soon as possible. We are starting to get backlogged. Do you see any problem with that?"

"No, Todd. That should be fine. Should I continue to schedule appointments on those days with Dr. Marks?"

"Yes, of course."

"No problem," I said.

"We will begin tomorrow. Let's say ten thirty."

I walked over to the human resources department. I wondered if Dr. Marks was aware that Todd had extended my hours. It had been less than a week, and I was almost back to full-time hours. I was exuberant. I stopped at the reception desk.

"John, you are a little early. Why don't you have a seat for a while?"

I sat down, picked up a magazine, and read an article on the top places to vacation in the United States. I was just finishing the piece when I heard my name being called. I looked up.

"You can go in now," the receptionist said.

Dr. Marks's door was open.

I walked into the office and sat down across from Dr. Marks.

"Good day, John. How is it going?"

"Couldn't be better," I said.

"Did you have a chance to practice with the tape?"

"Yes, but there was one slight problem." I looked up at Dr. Marks.

"What might that be?"

"I fell asleep."

We both laughed.

"Are you ready for phase two?" Dr. Marks asked.

"As ready as I could ever be," I replied.

"Okay then. I would like you to get into a comfortable position and close your eyes."

"Right now, Dr. Marks?"

"Yes, John. We are going to begin the exercise."

I closed my eyes and sat back in the chair.

Dr. Marks instructed me to take a deep breath.

After we completed the relaxation portion of the exercise, I was asked to show how relaxed I was with my finger. I rested my finger on the arm of the chair.

I was told to take a deep breath and feel a relaxing sensation traveling down my body from my head and face to my neck, shoulders, stomach, arms, and hands—and then my feet and legs. I was instructed to close my eyes and picture myself on the subway on 9/11. I elevated my finger.

Dr. Marks went through the preliminary relaxation exercise, and I relaxed again. He had me imagine walking through the train cars, and I raised my finger a little. He instructed me to take a deep breath and let it out very slowly. My finger went down. He had me imagine walking toward the Twin Towers and imagining the people and chaos. My finger went up high. He had me repeat the relaxation exercise several times, and each time I went through it, my finger dropped a little more until it rested on the arm of the chair.

Later in the session, Dr. Marks explained that he had to decide to either continue with the exercise or not. He was aware that I might have a major reaction to the imaginary situation. I might think about it anyway, which would make me more upset—and he might not be available to speak to me at that time. I had the tape, but what would happen if I was in the middle of an interview? Dr. Marks had confidence in the technique and my reaction to it. He decided to proceed.

"John, I would like you to picture yourself in front of the guard. Picture him telling you that you cannot enter the building."

My finger went up high, and Dr. Marks went through the relaxation exercise again. It took several times to reduce my anxiety.

"Now, John, you are walking out of the building."

My finger started to rise.

Dr. Marks repeated the exercise, and I lowered my finger and felt more relaxed. I was resting comfortably on the chair.

"John, picture yourself walking out of the building and hearing the thumping of people as they fall to the ground."

My finger elevated, my body stiffened, and a tear rolled down my face.

Dr. Marks repeated the exercise twice, and my finger remained elevated. The third time, my finger began to descend. It elevated one more time, and another tear rolled down my cheek. The source of the trauma had been tapped.

It took Dr. Marks an hour to help me work through my upset and distress.

When I opened my eyes, I felt like I had been to hell and back. I was sweating profusely, and my eyes were red. "That was so realistic, Dr. Marks. I felt like I was standing there again. Now that I am speaking about it, I am not as distraught. There is something to say about this treatment. I hope it lasts."

"John, you did well," Dr. Marks said. "You worked hard. Nice going."

I looked down at my body. My shirt was wet with perspiration, and my body was limp. "I have never felt this way before now. I am so relaxed!"

"A number of people have told me that, John," Dr. Marks said.

"That is good to hear. I thought I was overreacting."

"No, John. You did just fine."

I walked over to the window and said, "There are so many people in this city—each with their own special story. It is hard to imagine how each of us was affected by the events that unfolded." I turned and looked at Dr. Marks and then continued, "You and I each viewed those horrific events from different perspectives. Each of us has our own unique story to tell. How will we feel years from today? What will we tell our children and grandchildren? Just one day, in one moment in time, can have such an effect."

Dr. Marks nodded.

"I think it is time for me to go now, isn't it?"

"Yes, John. I will see you tomorrow. It will be later in the day. Have a good evening."

I guess he spoke with Todd.

I walked out of the office and looked up. The buildings were so tall, and I was so small in the scheme of things. I listened to the sounds of the cars and sirens. It was approaching rush hour when I walked into an alcove to call Christina.

"Hi, Christina. Sorry it is so late, but I just left Dr. Marks's office. It was an exceptionally long session today. I am exhausted."

After a long pause, Christina said, "Scott?"

"What? Oh, shit. I forgot. Scott and Lynda are coming over for dinner. Good thing we made it for seven thirty. I will be there as soon as I can."

I flagged down a cab, but I wondered if I could have arrived at Grand Central sooner if I had walked. I ran into the station and looked up at the display board. An express train was leaving in ten minutes. I hurried down to the track, stepped into the train, and took a deep breath of relief.

When I arrived in Milford, I ran to my car. I was glad that I had parked at the station that morning. I started the car and drove home. As I entered the house, I smelled chicken cooking. "I'm home."

"I am getting dressed in the bedroom," she said.

I entered the bedroom and kissed her. "I am going to shower. It was a tough session. I perspired, and the train was very crowded."

"No problem. You still have forty-five minutes. I will finish in the kitchen while you are getting ready."

I removed my clothes and placed the showerhead on vibrate. The warm water pulsating on my body felt so good. It felt like beads of effervescence were flowing down my back. I felt so refreshed. *I am looking forward to seeing Scott and meeting Lynda. Christina must have really fussed.*

I dressed and walked into the kitchen. "Christina, is there anything I can do to help?"

"No, John. I have everything under control. I even have some wine chilling in the refrigerator."

"You think of everything." I walked over and gave her a kiss.

"When I took your suit to the cleaners, you had a piece of paper in the pocket. I placed it on your dresser."

I went to the bedroom and unfolded the paper. It was Bill's letter of introduction. *I must have missed it when I removed his résumé from my pocket. I was supposed to contact the human resources department. I will bring the papers to work tomorrow. Now where did I put his résumé?*

I looked at the clock on the night table. It was seven twenty. I felt a little anxious, but I went back to the kitchen.

"John, everything is going to be just fine tonight. You do not need to worry."

"I know, but it is the first time I am going to see Scott since 9/11."

"Yes, John—and this is the first time he is going to see you."

The doorbell rang. "I will get it, Christina."

I opened the door. When I saw Scott and his wife, a chill ran down my body.

Scott looked at me, smiled, and introduced me to Lynda. "John, aren't you going to ask us in?"

"Sorry. Please come in. Let me take your coats."

I hung their coats up in the closet and said, "This is my wife, Christina."

"I would like you to meet Scott and his wife, Lynda."

Christina gave Scott a hug. "I feel like I know you. John speaks so highly of you. John, aren't you going to offer them a drink?"

"I guess I was consumed by the moment and forgot my manners. Of course I am. Would either of you like some wine? Christina is chilling some in the refrigerator."

Lynda said, "That would be nice."

Scott added, "I will have some too."

"I will get it then," I said.

Christina said, "Why don't we go into the living room? I have some cheese and crackers we can have before dinner is ready."

"Christina, you did not have to go to all that trouble. Didn't you work today?"

We walked into the living room and sat down.

As I entered the room, Lynda said, "No, you gave great directions—and we have GPS."

"Here we go," I said. "A white wine for you, Lynda, and one for you, Scott."

"John, I am so glad we were able to get together," Scott said.

I looked at him and said, "I have been looking forward to our visit as well."

"Lynda, would you like to see our house?" Christina asked.

Lynda placed her drink on the table and stood up. "That would be nice."

Scott said, "This is great cheese."

I looked at Scott and said, "I missed speaking to you. It has been a while."

Scott said, "If I lived closer to Orange, we would be able to hang out together. It's been a difficult time for me."

"I am sorry to hear that," I replied. "Oh, before I forget, here is the name of a doctor in New Rochelle."

Scott held out his hand. "Thank you, John. It is very much appreciated. I will call him in the morning. It could be very expensive."

"I can always help you out."

"John, that is very nice of you, but I will be fine. I have money left from my Christmas bonus, and I really need to speak to someone."

"Dr. Marks has been a major reason why I have been able to function. I was really hit hard by what happened."

"I know. I was able to tell that the first time I met you. You appeared shell-shocked."

"Really? I wasn't aware."

"We never are."

"Scott, you never told me what happened to you."

"There is really not much to tell."

"What happened?"

"Are you sure you want to hear? You have been through enough to hear about my experience."

"No, really, Scott, I want you to tell me."

Scott indicated that he was sitting in his office and was able to see the World Trade Center. It was just a coincidence that he saw the plane fly into the building. He was horrified. He thought a plane went off course, and it was an accident. People ran into his office to see what had happened. They also saw the second plane hit the second tower. "It was unbelievable." He was at eye level. Then the building shook. "We were all told to evacuate." When he got to the street, the first tower collapsed. He was several blocks away. There was soot and debris all around him. Scott was noticeably upset. His face was red, and he was holding his head in his hands.

I looked at him and waited for him to continue.

Scott stated that he tried to make his way home, but as he was walking down the avenue, he had looked back.

I said, "I know. I know. You saw what I did."

"Yes, John." Scott's hand started to shake, and he indicated that he couldn't get the site out of his mind. Scott began to tear up.

I placed my hand on his shoulder. "It will be all right. That is what I have been working on with Dr. Marks."

"Right now, it doesn't seem that way, John."

"I know. I felt the same way, but with each passing day—with the right treatment—it does get better. You need to believe me."

They looked up at each other.

Scott said, "Thank you, my friend."

"You never have to thank me. I will always be here for you."

"You are a good friend, John."

"Scott, that is what friends are for."

Scott stood up, shook my hand, and gave me a hug.

Christina and Lynda walked back in the room.

Lynda said, "Are we interrupting anything?"

Christina looked at John and then back at Lynda. "They were probably just having a moment."

"Just a friendly men's hug," I said. "We are starving. Is dinner ready?"

"John, it is a good thing you said something," Christina said. "Why don't you bring Lynda and Scott into the dining room?"

"This way—and bring your drinks," I said.

We sat down at the table, and I assisted Lynda with her chair.

"What a gentleman," she said.

"John, you are not setting a good example for me," Scott said jokingly.

Christina brought in a tray with four bowls of soup and placed them carefully on the table.

"This looks very good," Lynda said.

"Thank you," Christina said as she sat down at the table.

"So, Lynda, what keeps you busy during the day?" I asked.

"When you have three children, that is a full-time job. We were fortunate to have a free evening to join you. It took a lot of maneuvering to get us here. You will soon find out when you have children. You think it is difficult when they are first born, but as they grow, it becomes more demanding—sports, religious school, play dates, school functions, and doctor appointments. I could go on forever. It never ends. It is hard for Scott to share in the activities because he works such long hours in New York. You will see what I mean soon enough."

I thought, *I am sorry I asked. She seems so overwhelmed and not supported by her husband.*

Christina said, "Scott, what are names and ages of your children?"

"Judy is eight, Scott Jr. is ten, and Melissa is thirteen," Scott said.

"Christina, do you work?"

"Oh, yes, Scott. I work in marketing. My company just signed with a large account, and I am responsible for managing it."

"What do you actually do?" Scott asked.

Christina stated that she was accountable for the distribution of products around the world.

"That must keep you busy. What are you going to do when you have children?"

Christina looked at Scott and Lynda and smiled. "I have not really decided, but I will take maternity leave for a month. After that, we'll consider placing our child in day care for a few days. My mother might help out for a couple of days."

We had not spoken about childcare yet.

Lynda looked at Christina and said that when Melissa was born, she used day care, but when the other children were born, it was virtually impossible to juggle everything. She had to give up her job.

"What was that?" Christina asked.

Lynda was an administrative assistant at a bank and was in line for a promotion.

"Oh, that's nice."

"Staying at home really didn't do it for me, but I had no other choice. I did not want our children to be left alone after school—and they were too old for after-care programs."

Christina said, "John, why don't you tell them how we met?"

"I had several friends who wanted to fix me up, and Christina had the same. They thought we would make an interesting couple and gave me Christina's telephone number."

Christina collected the empty bowls and proceeded into the kitchen.

I said, "When I first called her, I did not think it was going to work."

"Why not?" Lynda asked.

"She was so sarcastic. I thought she would be a major challenge to date, but there was something special about her that intrigued me."

Christina came back with a platter of chicken, string beans, and potatoes. "Excuse me, John. Everyone, help yourselves."

I said, "When we met, it was love at first sight."

Christina sat down, and I helped her with her chair.

She smiled.

I said, "I think Christina felt the same way. We went for coffee and must have spoken for hours. It was wonderful."

Scott smiled.

Lynda looked up. "This is good, Christina. You outdid yourself. How did you find the time?"

Christina said, "It was nothing—just something I pulled together. Really, it did not take too much work."

"Scott, why don't you tell them how we met?"

Scott looked down at his plate, and his face turned red.

Lynda said, "Scott, go ahead and tell them. It is an interesting story."

Scott remained silent.

"Okay then," Lynda said. "I will tell them. We met in high school. I was smitten with him, but Scott paid me little attention. One evening in our senior year, we were at a party. We were drunk and hooked up. Nine months later, we graduated, married, and had Melissa. She was our love child."

There was dead silence at the table.

"Would anyone like another glass of wine?" I asked.

Lynda said, "I already had several, and another won't make too much of a difference.

"None for me," Scott said. "I am driving." He whispered in his wife's ear, but she kept holding her glass up.

When we finished dinner, we returned to the living room. I thought it best not to offer an after-dinner cordial.

Christina brought out a tray of coffee and cakes.

"These look good," Lynda said. "What are they?"

"It is my mother's recipe. They are her seven-layer cookies. Have one."

"They are good," Lynda said.

"What would you like in your coffee?" Christina asked.

"Just black for me," Lynda said.

"I'll have two sugars and cream." Scott bit into his cookie.

Lynda said, "Scott, you should be mindful of your weight. Remember what the doctor said. You need to shed some pounds."

Scott looked down and placed the seven-layer cookie on his plate.

Christina and I looked at each other, but we remained quiet.

Scott looked at his watch. "It is getting late. We ought to be going soon."

Lynda looked up at him and said, "Yes, you have to get up early to make the children's lunches and go to work."

Scott stood up. "It has been a delightful evening. Thank you for cooking for us. Your house is beautiful."

"I guess he is ready." Lynda put down her cup and stood up.

"Perhaps we can do it again sometime," Christina said.

"That would be nice." Scott gave Christina a kiss and shook John's hand.

I gave Lynda a kiss on the cheek.

She said, "Thank you."

"Good night—and thank you again," Scott said as he walked out the door.

Christina closed the door. "Wow."

"Yes, I know what you mean," I said.

Christina said, "They are some couple. Scott is a real nice guy, but Lynda is something else."

"Maybe it was the alcohol that brought out the worst in her."

"John, you are too kind. She is not a very nice woman, and she has a tremendous amount of anger. They really need to talk to somebody. There isn't one considerate bone in her body."

"Aren't you being a little harsh?"

"John, you are too forgiving."

"Scott is sitting there all embarrassed, and she goes into detail about how Melissa was conceived. She entrapped him—and now she is sorry she did."

"Christina, you are terrible." I began to laugh.

"What is so funny?"

"You are."

"You go on and on. Enough said. I really feel bad for Scott. He is a kind, gentle soul. I hope the therapy will open his eyes and give him some comfort. He certainly isn't going to get it from home. What is this about your mother?"

"I thought I told you. I must have forgotten. My mother volunteered to take care of the baby a few days per week."

"That is very nice of her. I would like that."

"I knew you would."

"She will really be good, and she lives on the way to your work."

"Yes, that is what I was thinking."

"Come over here and give me a kiss."

Christina hugged me. "I am so happy for us."

"I appreciate what you did tonight. I know it was hard to do the shopping and preparing when you are working so hard."

"John, I know how much Scott means to you. I can see why you like him. He seems very likeable."

"Let's clean up quickly."

"Why? What did you have in mind, John?"

I raised and lowered my eyebrows several times.

Christina said, "That would be nice."

I washed the dishes, and Christina stacked them in the dishwasher. When we finished cleaning the kitchen, I winked at Christina.

We walked to our bedroom.

I unbuttoned my shirt and took off my pants.

Christina changed into sexy lingerie and sprayed perfume on her long slendor neck.

I removed my socks, undershirt, and boxers.

Christina entered the room and dimmed the lights.

"You are so gorgeous."

Christina stood beside the bed; I could see her firm breasts through her sheer lingerie. She slowly approached.

I was excited. My chiseled torso and thin waist had not changed since we met. I was aroused and erect.

She sat down on the bed and massaged my legs. Her smooth hands moved in a circular movement to my thighs.

It felt so good.

She placed my engorged penis in her mouth and moved back and forth on me. At times she stopped and encircled me with her warm tongue.

I inserted my hand in her. She was moist and hot. She groaned with delight. She moved closer and kissed me.

Our tongues were pleasuring each other.

She climbed on top and sat on me.

I inserted myself into her, and we moved in perfect unison.

"Now, more," she yelled.

I was deep inside of her. I tried to hold myself back, but then I felt myself go.

She moved with a deep thrust, and as my hot fluid filled her, she yelled, "Yes!" She fell on top of me in pure ecstasy.

We slept in each other's arms.

When the morning came, we changed the sheets, showered together, and got dressed for work.

CHAPTER TWENTY-THREE

SIX MONTHS LATER

Days turned into weeks, and weeks turned into months. Christina was getting larger, and she was becoming increasingly more tired with each passing day. Medical appointments went well, and she had several ultrasounds. It had been confirmed that she was carrying a boy. Christina and I were busy, working hard at our jobs. I was now full-time. At times, it was necessary for me to stay at the office longer hours to fulfill my responsibilities. My appointments with Dr. Marks were once weekly. I was working through the trauma of 9/11. The frequency of nightmares and flashbacks had significantly decreased. I had interviewed and hired thirty new people and established three teams. Christina's new account was impressed by her performance, and she had been promised a promotion.

While I was on my home from New York City, Christina felt contractions. She called the doctor, and he was still in the office. She called Gina, and they rushed over to Dr. Stern. I met them at the doctor's office.

Christina was scared and frightened. The contractions had stopped, but she did not know what to expect. I arrived just as she was entering the examining room. We were both anxious and did not know what to expect.

"I am glad Dr. Marks had an emergency and was unable to meet with me." I took Christina's hand and gave her a kiss. "Don't worry, sweetheart. The doctor will be in soon."

Dr. Stern walked into the examining room and smiled. "You have been having contractions today? Can you describe them?"

Christina went into detail about what she was experiencing and how long each contraction lasted.

Dr. Stern said. "What has your activity level been during the past twenty-four hours?"

Christina looked up at Dr. Stern. "Last night, we went to bed ..."

"And?" Dr. Stern said.

"Well, we did have intercourse."

"How did you feel afterward?"

She said, "No different than usual."

"Did you reach orgasm?"

She smiled and nodded.

"Were you on your feet a lot today?" Dr. Stern asked.

"Yes. I had several presentations and lifted a heavy box or two."

"A box or two?"

"Maybe there were four," Christina said.

"Have you had any discharge or staining?"

"No, Dr. Stern."

"Mrs. Sable, you are entering your eighth month." Dr. Stern asked Christina to lie down on the examining table. He lifted her shirt and lowered her pants so that they were below her abdomen. "I am going to examine you." He put on his gloves and then applied the gel on her stomach and positioned the monitoring device.

"That is cold," Christina said as her body stiffened.

"There he is. Your healthy little boy does not appear to be in distress. That is a good thing. I am going to do an internal now. Your cervix is fine and appropriate for entering your eighth month." Dr. Stern handed Christina several paper towels. "Christina, you look like a nervous wreck. Let me assure you that everything is all right. Premature contractions are quite normal. You need to be a little more aware that you are close to your eighth month. I don't want you to lift anything over five pounds. Just ask someone to give you a hand at work. John, you will have to do your part too. Let's limit the intercourse for a few weeks and see if it makes a difference."

"No problem, Dr. Stern."

Dr. Stern, "I know you are the type of husband who helps around the house."

"Yes, sir."

Dr. Stern said, "Christina, I want to see you again next week unless the contractions persist. Do not worry about anything. I am around day and night. You can call me if you need to speak with me." He gave her his cell number.

Christina thanked him and said that she was feeling more relaxed.

"That is a good thing. Keep moving forward. Any questions?"

Christina asked if there were any other restrictions for driving or going to work.

"You certainly can go to work and drive," Dr. Stern replied.

Dr. Stern said. "Just go enjoy yourselves. In another month or so, you are going to be proud parents. Have you decided on a name?"

"No, not yet," Christina said. John nodded no.

"That's a good task for the both of you. See you next week," Dr. Stern said.

Christina summarized the session for her mother on the way to the car.

I said, "Christina, we have two cars. Do you want to stop for dinner? How about that place near your mother's? She can join us. Let's meet there."

"That sounds good, John," Christina said.

"No, you two should be alone. Just drop me off at home."

"No, Mom. I insist," I said.

Christina and Gina drove to the restaurant together.

After dinner, I drove Gina home, and Christina went home by herself.

"Thanks for taking Christina to the doctor."

"I am glad I was able to help." Gina said. "Good night, John, and thanks for the ride."

"Always my pleasure."

"Please wish Christina the best."

On the way home, I thought about Christina. *I will have to work fewer hours for the next couple of months and help out more around the house. I have been working long hours, and that has placed more responsibility on Christina. Perhaps I can do the food shopping on the weekends and cook some dinners and freeze them. We can eat on paper and try to go to bed earlier. I need to refrain sexually.* I pulled into the driveway, and the garage door opened.

Christina said, "I thought I would shower and get undressed. I hate the feeling of that gel on me. I am going to watch some television."

I gave her a kiss. "I am glad the two of you are all right." I set the table for breakfast and placed a load of laundry in the washer.

"John, what are you doing?" Christina called out.

"I thought I would put a load in the washing machine before I showered."

"There is no need for you to do that. I could have done it tomorrow."

"No problem. It is already done. Would you like some decaffeinated tea?"

"John, could you come over here? I would like to say something."

I walked into the family room. "Yes, Christina?"

"John, as you know, Dr. Stern has only placed two restrictions on my behavior."

"But—"

"There are no ifs, ands, or buts." She repeated herself, "There are only two restrictions placed on my behavior. Please do not treat me like I am handicapped. Do you understand?"

"Yes, Christina. I want to help out. You will need me to do things, especially after the baby comes."

"Thank you, John. Go shower, and we can meet in the living room."

After my shower, I joined Christina on the couch. "How about names, Christina? Have you given it any thought?"

"Have I given it any thought?" She laughed, reached over to the table, and picked up a book. "Look at this."

I looked down and gazed at the book title: *A Thousand Names for Expectant Parents.*

"This should help—or will it?"

"I know what you mean." I sat back on the couch and began to flip through the pages. "Christina, looking at these names will drive me crazy. Do you like any boy's names?"

"I was thinking," Christina said.

"Yeah, don't keep me in suspense." I laughed. "Let's see. I like Steven, Mark, Charles, Keith, and John. And you?"

"I have not given it much thought, but I guess I like Troy, Matthew, Zach, and William," Christina said.

"Those are all nice names," I said

Christina said, "Then let's consider the names from both lists. There are only nine names. I did not know you wanted to consider John as a name. If that is something you want, I guess that is what it should be."

"Christina, wasn't Charles your father's name?"

"Yes, but what does that matter? Your father's name was Timothy."

"If we start naming the children that way, we will need to have half a dozen children."

"That would be nice."

"Yes—nice and expensive. Remember each child means college education and support."

"Christina, you are too practical."

"And you are too romantic."

"You can never be too romantic."

Christina reached over and felt the inside of my leg. "You run hot, John." She moved her hand up and down my thigh.

"Please don't start anything. We are supposed to refrain."

"John, I am—but that doesn't mean you have to stop enjoying yourself." She smiled and grabbed me.

"Christina, that feels so good."

She moved her hand up and down.

My face turned red, and I kissed her.

She continued her hand movements as we kissed.

I moaned and said, "I'm going to come."

Christina placed her mouth over me and captured my bounty.

She ran into the bathroom. When she returned, she said, "John, that was some load. You are so powerful. It will give me something to look forward to in several months."

I looked at her and smiled.

CHAPTER TWENTY-FOUR

WORK AND THERAPY

"John, Mr. Lawson would like to see you." The door to Todd's office was open, and I walked in and sat down.

Todd was reading a journal at his desk. "I want to apologize for missing our meeting yesterday. I was called out of the office."

"That actually worked out for me because Dr. Marks also canceled—and I was called home for a medical emergency."

Todd stood up and closed the door. "Is everything all right?"

"Yes. Christina had to go to the doctor's office, but things went well."

"I am glad to hear that." He sat down beside me. "You have been working long hours here lately. If you need some time, feel free to take it."

"Thank you for the offer," I replied.

"How are you doing, John?"

"All right."

Todd looked straight into my eyes and said, "No, John. Really, how are you doing?"

I realized what he meant and said, "I am really doing fine, but my friend is experiencing some difficulties. I am giving him advice."

"Is that the fellow who you suggested a psychologist for several months ago?"

I was surprised that Todd would remember that, considering how many things he had on his mind. "Yes, that is the man."

Todd said, “I hope he is on his way to recovery. If not, it could be very daunting.”

“I know what you mean. As far as I am concerned, things are good. I am managing the weekly visits well.”

“How are the teams progressing?”

“We are getting ready to launch. I will be spending time with them in the new office on the ninth floor. We are just waiting for the construction to end.”

Todd said, “I know what you mean. It seems like the renovation has taken forever. I tried to stay on top of the contractors, but they are still setting up the computers in the cubicles. By tomorrow, the space should be ready.”

I looked out the window and then back at Todd. “Thanks for keeping up with it. It feels a little cramped up here.”

Todd agreed with me.

“I arranged all the files and downloaded them. As soon as we are up and running, we can start.”

Todd sat back on his chair and asked if there was anything else he could do for me.

“No, we are under control.”

“Next week, you will have a lot to report. Can we meet over lunch?”

I said, “That sounds great. I shall look forward to that, Todd.”

As I exited the office, Todd’s secretary informed me that there was a call waiting for me. My stomach sank. “Please put it through to my office.”

I picked up the phone and said, “Hello? John Sable here.”

“I am sorry to call you at work, but I needed to speak to you.”

“Hi, Scott. For a minute there, I thought it was Christina. How the hell are you?”

“Not too good.”

“Scott, where are you?”

“I am sitting in my car at the office.” He sounded like he had been crying. I heard him blow his nose.

“Why? What happened?”

Scott stated that he went into work, and they told him they were having a massive layoff. He had to pack up his desk. He had no warning. He was wondering what he was going to tell Lynda. He did know how much more bad news he could take.

"Scott, it is not the end of the world. Let's talk about it. Did they offer you any severance?"

"Yes, six months."

"Then you will have six months to find another job."

"The job market sucks."

"You need to think more positively."

"We just hired thirty new people. There must be other companies that are doing the same thing. Do you have a headhunter?"

Scott said, "There is this guy I used to know, but that was five years ago."

"Maybe he is still around. When we hang up, I want you to call him. Is your company providing any outplacement services?"

"No," Scott said. "The company is financially strapped, and they are just hanging in there."

"Then you are lucky."

"Are you crazy?"

"No, at least you are getting six months of severance before they go under. Just be sure to use the money wisely. Don't piss it away."

Scott was breathing heavily. "I should probably hold onto the money and not give any of it to my wife to manage."

"Who handles the money in your house?" I asked.

"She does."

"Don't you think that might be a problem if you hold onto it?"

"No. I will just deposit money on a weekly basis as if I were getting paid."

"I guess you have to do what you have to do."

"She will just waste it away and then blame me for not working."

"You know the best way to handle her."

"I feel so demoralized. I've never been fired before."

"Scott, let me remind you. You have not been fired. The company is downsizing, and you were let go."

"No matter how you say it, I have been fucking canned."

"When do you see the doctor again?"

"Doctor? Who will have money for a doctor?"

"Scott, now is the time that you need him. You are still collecting your pay for six months."

"Yes, but after six months, I will not have any income except for unemployment."

"Maybe, with the right support from a headhunter, you will have another job. You need to think positively—or the process of finding another job will not work for you."

"You just do not understand." Scott began to cry.

"Scott, if there is anyone who can understand, it is I. I thought my whole life was going to disintegrate on 9/11, and I am a survivor. You can do the same thing. You have to hang in there. I am here to support you." I picked up a pencil and started to doodle on a pad.

Scott said, "I just want to leave and run far away!"

"You will find the strength, and I am here to help you. I believe in you. You helped me, and I am here for you," I said.

Scott sniffed several times. "I am trying."

"Then let's come up with a plan. I want you to call that headhunter, revise your résumé, and call the doctor for an appointment. Don't worry about the money for the doctor. You still have insurance, and I can always help with the copay. No matter what Lynda might say, believe in yourself—and repeat over and over again, I can do it."

"You know how Lynda can be?"

"Yes, Scott, it doesn't take a rocket scientist to see how she treats you, but this is not about her now. It is about you and what you need to do to survive. You have three beautiful kids who love you and need you."

"Thanks, John. I don't know what I would do without you."

"One more thing, Scott," I said.

"What is it?"

"Call me tonight. I want to know what progress you made. That is not a maybe—that is a definite. I want to speak to you tonight."

I hung up the telephone and felt bad for my friend. First there was

9/11, and now he was let go from his job. I hoped Scott would follow through.

I looked at my watch. It was almost four, and I had an appointment with Dr. Marks. As I walked out of the office, I could not stop thinking about Scott. *What is going to happen if Scott doesn't follow through? I guess that is what wanting to take care of everyone and making it my responsibility means. There is only so much I can do. The rest is up to him. He is such a nice guy. He just needs a break.*

I walked into the reception room and sat down. Shortly thereafter, I was called into Dr. Marks's office.

"How is it going, John?"

"It has been a long day for me. I received good news from Todd—and then I received a call from a friend who is in distress."

"Do you want to talk about it?"

I went into depth, and Dr. Marks listened. When I was finished speaking, I waited for a response.

Dr. Marks handed me some tea and told me that he thought I had the situation under control. He commented that I was trying to help Scott and seemed not to be blaming myself for his situation. Dr. Marks sat down next to me. "You can only do what you can do, and your words of support were probably appreciated. A person can move only as far as he or she wants to move. There seem to be a lot of variables in play. Directing him to speak to a professional was the right thing to do."

"Doc, I am so concerned about him. He is very special to me. Scott was responsible for my keeping it together on 9/11. I want to be there for him. I know I can help him."

Dr. Marks took a sip of his tea and said that he knew I wanted the best for my friend.

"All I can do now is wait for his call."

"It may not come," Dr. Marks said. "You need to prepare yourself."

"I have faith in him. I know he will call me. If he doesn't call, I have a responsibility to call him."

"A responsibility?"

"Yes, don't I?"

"What do you think?"

"He has a plan. I guess it is up to him to execute it."

Dr. Marks said, "That is right. If he chooses to move forward, he will. If he does not, there may be nothing you can do. You need to accept that—no matter how hard that might be."

"I need to wait."

"Do you believe that?"

"Mentally, I do. I am not certain if I have an emotional handle on it."

"Perhaps other things are getting in the way."

"What do you mean?"

"What do you think I mean?"

I thought for a while. I walked over to the window. The buildings shielded the sun. The massive structures stood like soldiers guarding the building. I walked back, sat down, and took a sip of tea. "It is my feelings for him, isn't it? He is like my brother. I cannot abandon him. My emotions always seem to get in the way. I can't let it cloud my thinking of what is best for him, can I?"

Dr. Marks was silent.

"I provided Scott the tools. He has to be the one to use those tools to his advantage. I can't do his work for him."

Dr. Marks nodded.

"Thank you, Dr. Marks. Today's session was a timely one."

Dr. Marks looked up and asked, "John, what is your good news?"

"We are launching the program tomorrow."

"That is great. John, it is about that time."

"Can we meet after the launch tomorrow?"

"Yes, of course we can."

I did not want to miss the 5:45 train. Christina was expecting me, and I did not want it to be a late evening.

When I arrived home, the table was set, dinner was warming up in the oven, and the house smelled like an Italian restaurant. I had stopped at Grand Central and picked up some freshly baked bread.

Christina had just entered her ninth month. I kissed her and asked how her day was.

"Nothing too exciting. Our client wants us to market several of their other products."

"That is great, Christina. That means more business for the company."

"Yes, it does—and more work for my team, which is already stretched pretty thin."

"Why don't they hire more people to assist you?"

"They say they can't afford it now."

"Your new client has brought hundreds of thousands of dollars into the company, and they can't afford it?"

"That is right. We have not even received our bonuses yet. It is getting very frustrating. I got a call from a headhunter today."

"Is that good?"

"It could be. It was from one of our competitors, but they are located in New Haven. It would be a longer drive. I'm concerned about the baby and day care."

"Christina, you do not need to think of that. Consider the opportunity. Your company had promised you a promotion and a bonus months ago, and you are still waiting. Maybe it is time to see the writing on the wall. You have nothing to lose if you go for an interview."

"In my condition?"

"There is nothing wrong with your condition. It is life. You are the same person whether you are pregnant or not. If the company discriminates against you because you are pregnant, then you wouldn't want to work for them in the first place. You want to be associated with a progressive company—not one that has their heads up their asses."

"You certainly are not lost for words," Christina replied.

"What is right is right, Christina. You are a special woman with talent. That is the issue—not little Johnny." I looked up at Christina and winked. "He will be well provided for whether you are working in Milford or New Haven. You know your mom is there for us if we need her."

"Oh, I forgot to tell you. The new company has day care on its premises, and for newborns, they supplement your salary."

"Christina, it is your decision, but you should think it over very carefully. My dad used to say, 'Strike while the iron is hot.' One never knows when an opportunity will come knocking at their door again."

"Do you think we can handle all the changes at one time?" Christina asked.

"Christina, when you have a concerned husband and family who are there to support you, yes, but the decision is yours. What do you have to lose?"

"I will think about it."

"I am here if you need to speak to me about it."

"I know that, and I am grateful." Christina walked over and gave me a kiss.

The telephone rang.

I said, "I am expecting a call. I will get it. Hello? No, we are not interested in a free vacation. Please take our name off your list."

"Don't you hate that, John? When I was waiting to hear from you on 9/11, a telemarketer called. I was so disappointed and angry. Who are you waiting to hear from?"

"Scott was let go from work today. His firm said they were having cutbacks. He was in bad shape. I asked him to call me tonight."

"Why don't you give him a call and tell him you just got home?"

"I don't think that would be a good idea. We had a lengthy conversation at the office, and I suggested several things for him to do before he called me. If I call, he might feel I am checking up on him, and if he did not do what I recommended, it would put me in an awkward position."

"That makes sense. Let's have dinner. I am famished."

I said, "You sit, Christina. I will serve you."

"There is no need for that."

"I know, but I want to do it for the woman I love."

"John, what am I going to do with you?" Christina walked over and kissed me.

"Christina, in a few weeks, we will be parents." I raised my eyebrows up and down.

Christina smiled. She had prepared meatballs over penne pasta on Sunday and had frozen it. I took out the casserole and bread and brought it to the table. I served Christina and then myself. I ripped off a piece of bread and began to butter it. "I love the bread from this bakery. It is so fresh." I dipped it into the sauce and took a bite.

Christina took a bite of pasta and meatball.

I looked at Christina and said, "You should have been an Italian cook. You made enough for three meals too. Thanks, Christina."

I was washing the dishes when the telephone rang.

Christina waddled over to the telephone. "Hello. Oh, hi, Scott." She motioned for me to come to her. "It is for you."

"Thanks, Christina. Hi, Scott. I was thinking about you. I am glad you called."

Scott had called the headhunter and gotten several leads. He even had an interview in the morning.

"That is great, Scott. I forgot to ask if you wanted me to give your résumé to my human resources department. I gave them one for a friend several months ago, and they were able to place him. He is doing well."

Scott wanted to see what came of his interview first—and then he would let me know.

"That will be great."

Scott had called the doctor and had an appointment in two days. He had to update his résumé for the interview.

"That is great, Scott. You made my day. How about Lynda?"

"That is another story. She is a fatalist, and I do not have the strength to deal with her. I am trying not to listen to her. She is negative, and I am not letting her get me down."

"That's my boy," I said.

After he secured employment, he was going to find a good marriage counselor. If Lynda would not go with him, he would need to consider other options. He was beginning to realize that she made him feel terrible. If there is something 9/11 taught him, it was that life was too short.

"Scott, I am proud of you."

Scott said that he was proud of himself too. He had a revelation when we last spoke. He felt like a born-again person. His purpose in life was to move forward—at the very least—for his kids. He must think about them.

"I am glad you turned the corner, Scott. Be sure to keep me in the loop. I am interested and want to know what happens."

If things didn't work out tomorrow, the headhunter had told him that a guy with his education and experience would probably find something in less than six months. He wished me a good night and asked me to give Christina a kiss for him.

"I sure will. Good night." I hung up and gave Christina a kiss. "That is from Scott."

"Is he doing better?"

"Yes. In fact, he really sounded elated. You would think he was on something."

"Does he use?"

"I don't think so. He just had an uplifting conversation with his headhunter. He assured him that he would find a job within six months. He also set an emotional boundary with Lynda."

"That is good. It's about time."

"You are right. I hope she does not crush his positive energy."

Christina said, "I guess that is always a risk."

"I believe he will not let her this time. It is getting late, Christina. I think we should go to bed."

"Yes," Christina said. "I am pretty tired. It was a long day. I will meet you in the bedroom. I want to look at something in my wallet first."

CHAPTER TWENTY-FIVE

TOO MUCH TO BEAR

The telephone rang at five, and Christina answered it. "Hello?"

"It's Lynda."

"Oh, I did not recognize your voice. You have to excuse me. Do you want to speak to John? John, wake up."

"Christina, not now," I said.

"John, please wake up."

"What is it?" I asked.

"Lynda is on the telephone."

"What time is it?" I said.

"Five."

"Hand me the phone."

"Hello, Lynda. What's up?"

"Scott left the house last evening after we had some words."

"Was he upset?" I asked.

"Yes. He was agitated," Lynda said. "The police were just at our house. They found his car, and it had hit a tree."

"What?"

"He is dead!"

"Oh no. How could that have happened?" My eyes began to tear. "I can't believe it. I can't believe it." I handed the telephone to Christina.

"Lynda, how are the children?" Christina asked. "You have not told them yet?"

I sat at the edge of the bed and cradled my face with my hands.

"Please let us know when the funeral services will be," Christina said. "It might take several weeks to determine the cause of death. Well, if there is anything we can do, please give us a call. Goodbye." Christina hung up the telephone.

I looked up with tears streaming down my face. "That bitch drove him to it. She is a nasty person. I wanted to slap her."

"John, isn't that a little harsh?" Christina said.

"Scott is gone. I will never be able to speak to him again. It was just too much for him to deal with at this time. Why him? He was such a good person." I looked at Christina. "How are you doing?"

Christina said, "He was a nice, decent man. He will be missed." She put her hand on my shoulder. "You need to pull yourself together. Today is the launch of your department—and you will be needed."

I wondered how I would be able to go to work. *Scott is dead.* I felt a morbid feeling taking over my body.

Christina walked over to my side of the bed and looked into my eyes. "You have to carry on because today is important to you—and the company. It is something you have been working toward for six months. You owe it to your coworkers to be there for them. It is essential that you pull yourself together. This was a tragic event, but you did all you could."

"Christina, you don't understand. It is like a family member is gone. I felt so close to him. The thought of Scott not being in my life is too much for me to deal with at this moment."

Christina said, "I understand how you feel about Scott, but you need to move on. Life is that way. You never know what it might throw your way. Things happen, and there is nothing that can be done to bring him back." She reached over and gave me a hug.

I did not react.

Christina suggested taking a shower while she fixed us breakfast.

I continued to sit on the edge of the bed with my hands over my face.

Christina took my hand. "You are too big for me to move. Please stand up."

I looked at her hopelessly.

She stared into my eyes and said that I needed to consider her and the baby.

I looked back at her and walked robotically into the bathroom. I looked in the mirror and wondered what Dr. Marks would say. He would say, "John, you need to take hold of yourself. Scott did what he had to do, and you cannot take responsibility for his behavior. You need to grieve his death without destroying all that you have accomplished. It will be difficult, but you can do it."

After forty-five minutes, Christina knocked on the bathroom door and asked if I was all right.

I emerged from the bathroom in a much better state of mind. I was concerned about Christina and the baby. I should have considered Christina and not just myself. It was wrong of me to withdraw into myself. I walked over to Christina and gave her hug and a kiss.

Christina smiled and told me that it would be all right. "You reacted appropriately for what happened. Keep Scott in your heart and move on. Let him still be there as one of your supports."

I took comfort in knowing that Christina would be there for me.

CHAPTER TWENTY-SIX
THE LAUNCH

I got to work on time. It was a difficult morning, but whenever I felt upset, I placed my hand on my heart and smiled. I heard Christina's words and knew that somewhere, somehow Scott was there for me.

Everyone was excited about the launch of the new office. It seemed as though it was a new beginning, and they were placing the terror and horror of 9/11 behind them.

Todd said, "You did a marvelous job. You should be proud of your accomplishment."

Todd introduced me to several representatives from corporate headquarters. At ten o'clock, we rode the elevator to the ninth floor. There was a ribbon across the door.

Todd said, "You have the honors this morning. Please cut the ribbon."

I snipped the ribbon into two pieces.

The people on the other side of the door yelled, "Congratulations."

I placed my hand on my chest and smiled.

Todd said, "Who would have thought six months ago that this could be accomplished."

The men from corporate walked over and praised me.

The three teams walked through the glass doors and sat in their cubicles.

Todd said, "We have something special to show you. Please follow us."

We walked over to an office with windows that overlooked the city.

Todd said, "This is for you—and it is very much deserved."

I turned to Todd and said, "This is more than I could have wished for. Thank you. I appreciate your support and the confidence you have placed in me."

"Wait, John. I am not finished." He pointed to the door. There was a nameplate with my name and "vice president." I was speechless and held my hand to my chest.

"Are you all right?" Todd asked.

"Yes, Todd," I said.

"Let me formally congratulate you," Todd said. He held out his hand.

I shook it and said, "I appreciate everything you have done for me."

Todd smiled. "By the way, the promotion comes with an increase in salary."

"Wow."

"Enjoy it. You worked hard and deserve it. It is time for you to get to work."

"Yes, sir."

Todd smiled.

The day was full of excitement. There was heightened energy in the office. My staff really liked the new offices. I was able to look out at my staff from my office, and the staff could see me through the glass.

The work productivity was high that day, and I was certain that it would be true for the days that would follow. The staff enjoyed the new work environment.

I was looking forward to my appointment with Dr. Marks. It couldn't come soon enough for me. I walked into the doctor's office with an agenda. I looked at Dr. Marks and said, "This has been a very emotionally turbulent day for me."

"What do you mean?" Dr. Marks asked.

"Scott hit a tree and died. I am very upset and distraught. I feel like I lost a brother. I considered him a good friend, and I will miss him. Christina and I spoke for a long time. Scott is gone, but I must move forward with my life. It is important to be there for Christina and the baby. There are also other people who depend on me."

"I am so sorry to hear about Scott," Dr. Marks said.

I began to cry. "Scott was a very special person."

"Yes, he was," Dr. Marks, said.

"I do not know why he let that bitch upset him to the point of leaving. He told me that he was going to set boundaries and not let her upset him anymore."

"You sound angry?"

"Yes, I am damn angry." My face was red, and I held up my fist. "He let that angry woman get the best of him. I would like to slap her around."

"John, it is understandable how you feel."

"I can't get over it. I feel like I am having a bad dream."

"It does seem that way when we lose someone very close to us."

"That bitch. Why did Scott have to set foot in a car? Things were beginning to change for him. If he had just waited for a while, he could have had it all. I know I cannot take responsibility for his behavior, but I am still upset."

"That is understandable. It is going to take a while to heal."

"I know that I am wounded, but I will persevere. I have to worry about Christina and little Johnny. They should be my priority. I placed Scott in my heart. He is right here."

"John, you have made significant progress, and this incident might be like a setback. You lost a dear friend, and you should let yourself grieve. There are people around you who will support you. In addition, in the very near future, you will become a father. These are positive factors in your life that will propel you forward."

I looked up at Dr. Marks and said, "You are right. There are many things that I am thankful for in my life."

Dr. Marks nodded. "You said something good happened today?"

"Yes, today was the launch. The new office opened. It was well received by Todd and corporate. They even sent several representatives who congratulated me. You should see my new office. It overlooks the city. They really are taking good care of me. I was promoted to vice president and got a raise. I can't wait to speak to Christina. I tried to call her, but she didn't answer. She must be in a meeting. You know something, Doc, I couldn't have done it without your help."

Dr. Marks smiled.

"It is time for me to go, isn't it?"

"Please take care of yourself. I am truly sorry about your friend. See you next week."

I walked out of the doctor's office and was still very conflicted. It was a very hard day, and I was tired. I just wanted to speak to Christina. I tried calling her cell phone, but there was no answer. I called the house, but there was no answer. My phone buzzed. I had just received a text:

Sorry I couldn't take your call. I was in a meeting for most of the day.

Will speak later. xoxo Christina

I felt better after I heard from Christina.

When I arrived at Grand Central, I took a seat on the train. I leaned back, fell asleep, and started to dream.

It was raining hard, and I had just left the house. I was running an errand for Christina at the convenience store. It was hard to see through the windshield because the defroster was not working. I wiped the window with my hand as the traffic light turned red. I put the radio on, and they were playing a song I used to dance to in high school. I began humming, and the light turned green. The car behind me honked. *Everyone is in a rush*, I thought.

When I arrived at the store, the rain was heavier. I waited a few minutes, but it did not let up. I decided to brave it. I opened the door and made a run for it.

In the store, Scott was standing in front of me. I was surprised to see him there and gave him a hug. We began to exchange words.

Scott told me that he was going away and that he would not see me again.

I asked him to stay.

Scott insisted that he had to go.

I told him that I needed his friendship, and he had to stay.

Scott began to walk away. He turned back for a moment and said, "Everything will be all right. Keep me in your heart."

I began to cry and yelled, "Please don't go. Please don't go."

Scott said, "It is my time."

I said, "But Scott—"

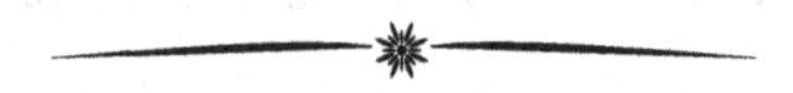

The train jolted, and I woke up.

A tear dropped onto my shirt. I wiped my face, took out a tissue, and blew my nose. I wanted to go back to sleep and see Scott again, but I knew that was not possible. I felt comforted from the hug. That would need to stay with me. I smiled and placed my hands on my heart.

When the train pulled into the Milford station, a light rain was falling.

I was looking forward to discussing my promotion with Christina. I entered the house and walked directly to the kitchen.

Christina was standing by the stove. She turned when I walked into the room. We greeted each other with a kiss. Her warm, moist lips comforted me.

"How was your day?" she asked.

"It was an emotional roller coaster."

"What do you mean?"

I began to explain my day.

"That was a nice surprise," Christina said. "How wonderful."

I placed my hands over my heart and said, "It felt like Scott was with me the whole day."

"That must have made you feel a lot better."

"Have you heard from Lynda?"

"No, but she did say it may take several weeks."

"I hope we hear something soon. My appointment with Dr. Marks also went well. He has been very helpful."

Christina remarked that Dr. Marks had been a great support for me.

I mentioned that I had been talking her ear off and asked about her day.

Christina said, "There is something I wanted to discuss with you."

I said, "Should we sit down?"

"Not unless you will be more comfortable," Christina said. "Remember yesterday—"

"Yeah, it seems like it was week ago."

"Our discussion about the headhunter?"

"Oh, yes."

"I called the headhunter's office this morning, and they wanted to speak to me. I set up a lunch meeting."

"And?"

"They offered me the job and really want me to join the firm. They were willing to wait until a month after we have the baby."

"And?"

"The office is located in New Haven, and I would be responsible for several large accounts. The responsibilities are somewhat greater—but so is the salary. The perks are unbelievable, including childcare and four weeks of vacation!

"That is great, Christina. Are you going to take the job?"

"I have to give two weeks' notice. I'll also take several weeks off before we have the baby. That would give me time to fix up the baby's room and do some other things in preparation for the big day. I want to be sure that you support what I want to do."

"It's a great idea." I gave her a hug and kiss. "Scott really is looking out for us. Let's celebrate by going out for dinner!"

"You know me—you don't have to ask me twice," Christina said.

"What do you feel like eating?"

"Let's see. How about Italian?"

"Do you want to call Mom and ask her to join us?"

"That would be nice," Christina said. "Hopefully she hasn't eaten yet."

I called Gina and asked her to join us.

"Mom is going to join us."

"That is great."

We shared our news over dinner. There was a somber moment when we discussed Scott, but I was in a better place.

We returned home and went to sleep.

CHAPTER TWENTY-SEVEN

THE BIG DAY

Time was moving faster than we realized. It was close to nine months after 9/11, and the media was still replaying the events almost daily. Christina and I were busy preparing for the birth of our child. Christina had given her notice and was keeping herself occupied around the house. Her suitcase was packed, and Gina was on high alert. I was busy at work, and the days flew by.

I woke up, showered, and dressed for work. I had an unsettled feeling and wanted to stay home. Other than feeling tired, Christina was doing fine. Her last appointment with Dr. Stern went well, and I really did not have any reason to feel alarmed. I decided to go to work and left Christina sleeping. I thought she needed the rest.

I was extremely restless on the train ride into New York. When I reached my office, I looked at the beautiful skyline. I had started to review the files on my desk when my cell phone rang.

"John, this is Christina."

"Are you all right?"

"I'm fine, but you ought to come home. The contractions have begun."

I told her I would leave the office immediately.

"Don't worry. They may stop. Take your time."

I called Todd and explained the situation.

He said, "Just go home."

I flagged down a cab and took the first train out of Grand Central.

The stress of thinking about Christina tired me out. I placed my head back on the seat, and the movement of the train soon put me to sleep.

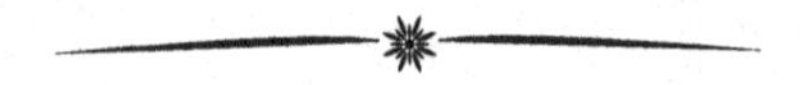

Christina was working around the house. Her contractions were increasing, but they were still mild. She called Gina.

Gina asked Christina if her water had broken.

"No, not yet."

Gina decided to come to the house and wait with her.

Christina told Gina that she was fine.

Gina said, "The contractions could increase at any moment—and you need a way to get to Yale New Haven Hospital."

When Gina arrived, Christina was making up the crib in the baby's room.

"Christina, call Dr. Stern and let him know what is happening."

Christina said, "I am doing well."

"Yes, but the doctor should know what you are experiencing. He may want to see you."

Christina said, "Perhaps you are right." She called the doctor. "Hello. This is Christina Sable. Is Dr. Stern available? He is in with patients? Could you tell him that I am having contractions?" Christina turned to Gina. "They said just a minute. Oh, hi, Dr. Stern. They started several hours ago. They are more regular now. I am not in any major distress. Oh, I see. My mother is with me. Yes, she drives. It should take us about fifteen minutes. See you there."

When Christina hung up, she explained that the doctor wanted to meet her at the hospital.

Gina asked Christina where her suitcase was and took two towels from the linen closet.

"What is that for, Mom?"

"Just something for you to sit on in the car."

On the drive to the hospital, Christina called John to explain the situation.

"Good thing you called, Christina. I will take the train right to

New Haven and take a cab to the hospital. I will be there as soon as I can."

When Christina arrived at the hospital, the staff was waiting for her. They had her insurance information on file and escorted her to a room. Gina followed her. They handed Christina a hospital gown and asked her to change. Christina felt a contraction and felt something wet.

"Christina, your water just broke," Gina said. "Here are some paper towels to dry off your legs."

"Thank you, Mother" Christina said.

Christina changed into the gown as a hospital attendant entered to clean the floor.

Dr. Stern popped his head into the room. "Christina, we are going to take a ride down the hall to one of the rooms for an ultrasound. The attendant will help you up onto the examining table."

As they rode down the hallway, Gina followed close behind.

"Let's take a look." The doctor exposed Christina's stomach, applied the gel, and obtained the image he wanted. "Your little fellow has not turned. He likes it in there. He is a big guy—probably a nine-pounder. Christina, I am going to do an internal now. Did you feel that, Christina? That was a contraction. Christina, your boy is breeched. I guess he wants to run out. We are going to prep you for a C-section. This is not unusual."

Christina began to cry. "Where is John?"

Gina said, "He is on his way. He should be here soon."

Dr. Stern turned to Christina and placed his hand over hers. "Christina, I assure you everything will be fine. We are just going to give you something that will put you to sleep so we can do the surgery."

They started her IV.

"I want you to count backward from one hundred. That's it—you are doing fine. Wheel her in, guys. She is ready."

A nurse said, "You must be Christina's mom. Could you please have a seat in the waiting room? I will come in and let you know how she is doing."

The train pulled into New Haven. I was thankful that it was on time. I was worried all the way to the station and did not know what to expect. I was afraid that something might go wrong.

I flagged down a cab.

When I entered the hospital, the staff had some difficulty finding Christina. They finally located her and sent me to the waiting area. They told me to follow the blue line to the last room on the right. I walked quickly down a narrow hallway. When I entered the room, I saw Christina's mom. I was glad to see her. "What are you doing in here?" I asked.

"Christina is in the operating room."

"What?"

"I did not want to alarm you, but the baby is breeched."

"What is that?"

"It never turned and was presenting feet first. They have to perform a C-section."

"A C-section?"

"Yes. Dr. Stern is in there now. He said he would let us know how things are going as soon as he can."

"How long ago was that?" I asked.

"About half an hour ago. It all happened so fast. Christina did not even want to call the doctor, but she was having contractions."

"It is nice that you were able to accompany her. I'm sorry I was at work."

"How were you to know?" Gina said.

"Yes, of course."

Dr. Stern entered the waiting area. "John, you are now the proud father of a nine-pound-two-ounce baby boy. Mother and baby are doing well. You can go into the nursery and get acquainted with your son."

I hugged Gina and gave her a kiss. I was ecstatic.

I walked hurriedly into the nursery. A nurse stopped me and

noticed that I was not wearing a nametag. She directed me to return to the main desk in the lobby.

Gina told the nurse that I was her son-in-law, but the nurse would not yield. She sent me back to the lobby.

It was like a maze, and I could not find my way. When I finally arrived, I was sweating profusely and annoyed. I tried to calm down, but it was pointless. When I finally got to the front of the line, I was handed a nametag.

I ran down the hallway and took the elevator to the maternity ward. The elevator stopped between two floors, and an alarm sounded. I was alone on the elevator and felt trapped. Several minutes later, it started to move. I arrived back in the nursery, and a nurse walked me over to greet my son.

I held him close and raised him above my head. "May you grow up in a world where hunger has ceased and peace dominates."

I was so proud of my newborn baby boy. After so much anticipation, baby Johnny was finally here.

Dr. Stern entered the nursery and asked to speak to me.

I handed the baby to the nurse, and she wheeled him away.

"What is happening?" I asked.

Dr. Stern placed his hand on my shoulder. He told me it was just a precaution, but the nurse had heard an irregular heartbeat during delivery. They wanted to evaluate the situation in the pediatric intensive care unit. I felt a knot in the pit of my stomach. "Does Christina know?"

"We were going to tell her after we spoke to you," Dr. Stern said.

I knew Christina would be out of sorts when she heard the news. "Let me walk with you, Doctor. I would like to be there when you speak with her."

We walked down the hall to her room. She had just been wheeled in from recovery.

"John, what is going on? Is the baby all right?"

"Nothing to be too alarmed about, Christina," Dr. Stern said. "We heard some irregular heartbeats during the delivery and have taken the baby to the intensive care unit to check him out."

"Check what out?" Christina asked.

"We have called in a cardiologist, and he is going to listen to your baby's heart. If he feels he needs further tests, an echocardiogram will be considered."

Christina said, "What's that?"

Dr. Stern said, "It is a diagnostic procedure where we take a look at the baby's heart. We will know more after we have had a chance to review all the information. Are there any heart problems in your families?"

I said, "No."

Christina looked at Dr. Stern, and a tear rolled down her check. "My father died of a heart attack."

Dr. Stern said, "I will share that information with the cardiologist, and I will speak to you as soon as we know something."

Christina began to cry. "My baby, my baby. When will I be able to see him?"

"As soon as we complete the evaluation." Dr. Stern placed his hand on her shoulder. "Don't worry. He is in the best of hands. I need to leave. I would like to be downstairs when they examine the baby." He turned and walked out of the room.

Christina looked at me and said, "Why is this happening to us? I can't understand."

I was extremely anxious, but I had to keep it together for Christina. "Christina, everything will work out for the best. I was just holding him in the nursery. He appeared all right to me."

"Yes, John, but you are no doctor."

"Christina, we have to be optimistic, and all we can do now is wait."

Christina wiped her eyes with a tissue. "I guess you are right."

It was two hours before we heard anything, but it felt like days.

Gina joined us in the room. We were all apprehensive, and I felt a tremendous sense of uncertainty. I was having a difficult time expressing myself.

Christina cried off and on.

Gina tried to interject some conversation, but it was to no avail.

Dr. Stern and another physician walked into the room. "Let me introduce you to Dr. Dolan. He is the cardiologist."

Dr. Dolan was at least six foot five. He was an attractive middle-aged man with gray hair and a mustache.

Christina sat up in bed and said, "Where is my baby?"

Dr. Dolan said, "That is what I am here to speak to you about. He is still in the intensive care unit."

Christina said, "What is he doing there?"

"It appears that he is suffering from a congenital heart defect."

Christina said, "Oh no!"

"Please let me continue. He will need surgery as soon as possible to correct the problem. His aorta is constricted and is not permitting the blood to flow freely. We have to operate and correct the problem. The procedure has been performed and perfected over the years. Unfortunately, time is of the essence. We will not be able to bring him to you at this time. We are waiting for the pediatric cardiac surgeon as we speak. He should be arriving momentarily. There are some forms you will need to fill out before the surgery. I realize this is a lot for you to process, but I will be back to speak to you at greater length a little later. Please write down your questions for me. I was just paged and need to go speak with the surgeon. I will speak to you later."

Dr. Stern said, "I am so sorry for both of you, but Dr. Dolan is right. This type of operation has been performed many times, and we are fortunate to have one of the best pediatric cardiac surgeons on our staff. You will get to meet him after the surgery. You will need to sign the papers to authorize him to perform the surgery."

Christina said, "This is all happening so fast. I guess we have no choice. If we do not sign, the baby's life will undoubtedly be at risk."

I shook my head.

We signed the papers, and Dr. Stern brought the documents to the other doctors.

Gina said, "We need to believe that everything will be all right. Sometimes these things just happen. It is in the Lord's hands."

I walked over to Christina and gave her a kiss and then a hug.

Gina smiled and said, "We just have to wait now."

Christina said, "All we seem to do around here is wait."

"Yes, but when they return, it will be over," I replied.

"It really is in the Lord's hands," Christina said.

We were hoping there would be news about the baby, but it did not come. The sun began to set, and there was still no word. Gina went to the cafeteria and brought back sandwiches for us.

At seven thirty, the doctors walked into the room.

Dr. Dolan said, "Let me introduce you to the cardiac surgeon. Dr. Mellon performed the surgery."

Dr. Mellon was a short, bald man with a deep voice. "Mr. and Mrs. Sable, the operation on your son went well. There were no complications. We will have a better idea in a couple of days. Right now, your baby is resting comfortably in the cardiac section of the pediatric intensive care unit. I must caution you that he is connected to an array of devices. It looks scary, but we need to monitor him very carefully. I will check in on him before I leave tonight, and a cardiac nurse will be monitoring him throughout the night. In my opinion, the worst is over. As he improves, the tubes and devices will be removed. I know you just had surgery, Mrs. Sable, but I told my staff to let you visit your son. For tonight, it should be a brief encounter for you and your husband. I will see you in the morning."

Two nurses appeared at the door with a wheelchair. "Mrs. Sable, we are here to take you to the intensive care unit. It will be just a minute. We have to bring your IV. Just sit up and turn your legs. Easy now. We are both going to help you up and place you in the wheelchair."

I walked over and offered a hand.

"No, Mr. Sable, that will not be necessary. We have everything under control. There you are, Mrs. Sable. You are ready. By the way, I am Joyce, and this is Cassandra."

"Thank you both for your help," Christina said.

"Don't mention it. That is what we are here for—to be of service to our patients. Now, Mr. and Mrs. Sable, your little fellow has been through a lot in the past several hours. He is in a delicate situation, and he is connected to an array of machines and tubes. It may be difficult for you to see him this way, but these are just monitoring systems. They are typical for the type of surgery he had. If you have any questions or concerns, please ask us."

The nurses wheeled Christina down the hall, and Gina and I followed them. It was nine thirty, and there were not many people around. I heard moans from one room, monitors in several rooms, and the wheelchair squeaking against the linoleum floor.

At the elevator, I said, "What floor are we going to?"

Cassandra said, "The eleventh floor is where the pediatric cardiology ICU is."

The doors of the elevator opened, and Christina was wheeled into the confined space. I followed Christina and her mother.

I was quite uncomfortable, and I felt a knot in my stomach. My face was flushed, and I began to sweat.

The doors opened, and I took a deep breath.

Several nurses were treating the children.

These poor little infants, I thought. *Why has life been so cruel to them? They are so innocent and have to fight these battles so early in life.*

Cassandra said, "We are sorry, but only one of you can go in at a time. We are going to wheel Mrs. Sable in first."

Gina and I stood together and waited.

Two nurses were standing by a bassinet that was surrounded by monitors and IVs.

Christina said, "Is that baby John?"

The nurses pushed her closer. "Here we are. There he is."

Christina reached over the side of the bassinet and touched his delicate fingers. A tear rolled down her cheek. "Why him? My sweet little boy, we will get through this together. We are here for you." She turned to one of the nurses. "How is he doing?"

"So far, so good. He is a tough little boy. He has been through a lot, but he is a fighter. In a few days, we should know more. Dr. Mellon is a remarkable man. He has performed many of these operations. Don't worry. In less than a week, you will be holding him. If you would like, you can express some of your milk so we can feed him when he is ready. The nurses will help you. It will also help with your healing process."

Cassandra said, "It is time for us to go. Your baby needs his rest." They wheeled her back to the opening of the partition.

I began to walk into the room.

"Sir, we have to accompany you."

I was excited to see my son. As I approached, I thought about holding him in my arms. It was just for a few moments, but his body was so warm. I had looked into his blue eyes.

Baby John was sleeping.

When I arrived at his bedside, my eyes filled with tears. I placed my arms in front of my stomach and looked down. I stood in silence for several moments, took a step back, and then motioned to the nurse that I was ready to return.

Gina was not permitted to enter the ICU unit, but she watched from the window.

When I returned, we went back to Christina's room. We were going to have to navigate through this somehow. I did not think I could ever feel worse than I had on 9/11. Once again, I was experiencing a terrible tragedy. *Will it ever end? Wasn't my parents' deaths and 9/11 enough? Why does it continue to happen to me? What the fuck did I do to deserve this?* I wanted to speak to Dr. Marks, but it was eleven o'clock. I did not feel it was right to disturb him. *I just have to work things out on my own. First, Scott—and now this? I am certainly being tested. Christina does not deserve this. She is a good woman, and she is kind, generous, and giving. She should not have to go through anything like this. I must be there for her.*

Christina and I looked at each other, and our eyes filled with tears.

Gina asked if I would like a ride home.

"No, Mom. I will sleep here in the hospital with Christina. I can stay on the recliner in the room. I will be more comfortable if I am here. If there is any news to report, I will call you. We will see you in the morning. Good night."

"Don't worry. I know everything will be all right." Gina gave Christina a kiss and me a hug and left the room.

I said, "Who would ever think that we would be in this situation?"

"I know. It was a perfect pregnancy. I was expecting everything to work out for us. Now look at us. I had surgery, and my little fellow has had surgery."

"Christina, we are all alone. We are here several floors away from our son. All we can do is pray and wait."

Christina said, "All I want to do is scream."

"I know how you feel. Actually, I feel like punching someone out."

"John, I've seldom heard you speak that way."

"I know, but I have never been in this situation."

Christina said, "I would like to run downstairs and pick him up and run out of this damn hospital."

"Let's do it," I said.

Christina looked at me, and I pulled the IV out of her arm. She grabbed her hand, and we ran to the elevator.

When we arrived at the ICU, a guard stopped us. "You cannot go in there."

"Yes, we can." I began to enter the unit.

The guard called for backup and grabbed me.

Christina screamed, "Stop! You are hurting him. Stop. He is the father, and he has the right to enter."

I punched the guard, but he placed me in a headlock.

Christina yelled, "Stop!"

The train came to a screeching stopped. My head jerked and hit the window. I woke up and felt completely disoriented.

The conductor yelled, "Next stop, New Haven."

Rubbing my head, I realized where I was—and where I was going. I felt a sense of relief. I thought, *Thank heavens it was only a dream!*

Printed in the United States
By Bookmasters